The Quest for the Tri-County Trophy
The Preseason

ERICH JOHANN HAAS

ISBN: 1517542545
ISBN 13: 9781517542542

For my son, Alex Von:

May he always stay aware of his surroundings.

ACKNOWLEDGMENTS

I want to thank my best friend and gift from above, my beautiful wife, Julie Ann.
She is a testament to the patience of life.

1

My name is Ricky "the Fridge" Cooper. I like to think I have the nickname "Fridge" for all the baseballs I eat up behind home plate, but there are others who would say it's because I know my way around a dinner plate. Either way, I accept "the Fridge." I'm a five-foot-eleven, solid, two-hundred-pound, seventeen-year-old senior at Beaver Falls High School in Crossroad County, where I play baseball for the Fightin' Beavers. My willingness to win, along with my stature and ability to command a team and control a game, puts me behind the plate as the catcher and team captain. This has been no easy chore, but one of the talents I possess is the ability to maintain focus on achieving my ultimate goals: winning and receiving the Tri-County trophy and getting to the next level of competition.

So let me brief you on what has led me up to this point. My parents, Mr. and Mrs. Cooper, got together early and took the opportunity to see life outside of Crossroad County. When they decided to start a family, they came back to their hometown. Soon after, Dad did his part and seeded the love of his life.

While waiting for my arrival, Dad, a barber by trade, bought a building on the northeast side of town and started a barbershop in Beaver Falls. We lived in the upstairs apartment for the next ten years. My mother was a schoolteacher, but she and Dad decided it would be best for her to stay at home with me until I was in grade school. Dad especially liked the idea of a short climb upstairs for a quick lunch and a glimpse of his wife who was carrying his soon to be game changer in life.

Early one spring morning, my eyes saw their first light. A twelve-pound baby boy slid out into the doctor's hands at Delivers Hospital. I guess Dad almost had the doctor talked into wearing a catcher's mitt during the delivery—until Mom, in a sedated state of mind, caught a glimpse of that dirty old mitt and said, "Absolutely not!"

Meanwhile, as everyone was astonished by my size, I was taken to the nursery for a cleanup and a start toward one of my life's pure joys: feeding time. They quickly realized they were trying to feed a twelve-pound bottomless pit. Two days later, they wished my parents good luck and sent us on our way.

Over the next couple of years, living atop the barbershop, I thought all kids lived like the Coopers: moms and dads always around, dads working downstairs from where you slept, and sports were the only thing on television. But the older I got, the more aware I became of my surroundings. I started to see a different picture.

First, not all boys around my age had a ball mitt constantly on their left hands. Also, not every kid played like I did. I was always throwing a ball with Dad or anybody waiting on a haircut. If there were no takers, I would bounce it off anything I could, including things I wasn't supposed to. Plus, I would pretend to be the best ball player ever to come out of Beaver Falls High: the great right-handed catcher, Louie Parker, a.k.a. "the Backstop."

The first time I remember meeting this icon was the last time the Tri-County trophy was escorted to Crossroad County and into Beaver Falls. It must have been those uniforms, along with the hoisting of the silver trophy, and everyone lining Main Street to cheer on the victors, which left an indelible impression in my mind. The sea of orange and black waved back and forth with the, "That's right!" kind of attitude and feeling of confidence that winners possess. That day, I made one of the finest plays of my life. I was five at the time.

The team was sitting atop a hay wagon pulled by Mr. Ferguson's field tractor. The Backstop himself was among them, tossing out plastic championship balls. My eyes fixed on the square-jawed catcher, still sporting his shin guards. He tossed one of those balls toward where we were standing outside the barbershop.

I never hesitated. Shaking off the loose grip that my dad had on my hand and taking a few steps forward, I watched the ball hit the pavement twice and knew the next time it came in contact with something, it would be the ball glove on my left hand. Watching it all the way in and squeezing the mitt shut, I looked up at the Backstop. Through all the cheering, clapping, and the hoorays for the champion Beavers, he shot me a wink and a thumbs-up. Shooting a grin back, I ran to my parents to high-five my dad, saying, "I want to wear shin guards." Laughing with pure pride, Dad picked me up and held me high as though I was his championship trophy.

Later on that evening, Dad finished up with his haircuts and came upstairs. Automatically, he yelled, "Stop standing there with the refrigerator door wide open, Ricky!" He mentioned a restaurant that was going to open in the old diner. Dad—of Irish and German descent—said excitedly, "They're going to name it 'The Irish Schnitzel.' They're supposedly going to restore it back to its original shape. And guess what Ricky? The folks running it have a son your age."

Closing the fridge door with a pudding cup in hand, I quickly asked, "Does he like baseball?"

Smiling at me, Dad replied, "We'll soon find out, son." Taking me by the hand, he said, "Now, let's go get you a catcher's mitt."

I could take you on the long journey of my childhood, but I'll save it for another time. This story is going to be about the quest I've been on since I stood outside the barbershop that summer day. Bits and pieces will be about growing up in Beaver Falls, but mostly this is going to take place my senior year on the veteran-loaded Fightin' Beavers baseball team. To get you up to speed, I have to tell you how our junior year ended.

It started with us losing in the Tri-County semifinal game against the Northwood Lumberjacks. It was a tough loss, but gloves down, the Lumberjacks had a better team. They were loaded with seniors, with a stud ace on the mound who hurled a complete game, giving up just one run.

That single run the Beavers put on the board came off the bat of yours truly, "the Fridge." During the top of the fifth inning, with the count 0 and 2 and two fastballs that caught the corners, I was sitting on the changeup and guessed right. Leaving the right side of the batter's box and watching the ball steadily climb into the light-blue sky, I quickly downshifted into one of the finest motions an individual can perform: the home run trot. After touching first base and heading toward second, I knew the baseball, resting under someone's sedan in the left-field parking lot, had just set the Fightin' Beavers' all-time season record for dingers. Brushing the excitement from my face, I quickly regained focus and rounded third. Like always, I got no high five from Coach and instead received his usual nod. I glanced back at the Lumberjacks' ace and was certain that was his last mistake of the game. Touching home, I turned to a mob of teammates who smacked my helmet and gave me fist bumps and an "Attaboy, Fridge!" and a whack across the rear end (that one I knew came from "Big Red" McStein).

But the rally was shortly out of outs. After seven innings and the umpire's final call of "Strike three!" on J. J., our hope of hoisting the Tri-County trophy came up a game and a half short. Losing is the only thing I have trouble swallowing.

However, as I walked through the line and slapped the hands of the victors, I was proud of our team. After all, unlike the Lumberjacks, we were mostly all juniors. With experience and raw talent at every position, and a few all-Tri-County players, I thought we would be bound to make an impact next season.

I walked back to our dugout with Big Red's arm draped over my shoulder. He gave me the kind of encouraging words that one would only hear from his best friend: "Hey, Fridge! Did you get a look at

THE QUEST FOR THE TRI-COUNTY TROPHY 5

the blonde sitting atop the bleachers? I tell you what, Fridge. I think she's teetering a possible ten."

Ah, classic Red. Always living in the present. If only I could possess a bit of his short-term focus.

"No, Big. I'm already looking forward to next year for another shot at the trophy."

"There you go again, Fridge, always game planning ahead. Besides we got a great group coming back next year with experience, and…"

"Ya. I know, Big, with experience and talent at every position."

"Yes, especially with you, Bo, and Lefty. Either way, Fridge, we got a hell of a summer to enjoy. So for now, forget about it and take a look at that beauty."

Already aware of the blonde that Red had rated so highly, I flashed a slight wink under the bill of my cap to the big guy. That's when Big Red remembered that Ricky Cooper was always a step ahead.

Coach Gibbs gave a short speech: "We'll get 'em next year, boys. Now pack it up." Some of the teammates congratulated me on the new homerun record. Just then, our young bat boy, Billy, came up to me.

"Mr. Cooper?" he asked in his shy, shaky voice.

I turned to face the young lad. "Billy, how many times do I have to tell you? Call me 'Ricky' or 'Fridge' or even 'Cooper.'"

He gazed at me goggle eyed. "Mr. Ricky 'The Fridge' Cooper?"

I couldn't help but laugh at the boy for his idolism. "Yes, Billy?"

"Um, there is a guy standing on the other side of the dugout that…uh…wants to talk to you, and…uh…Bo."

"Ok, Billy." Before I turned away, I reached in the side pocket of my bat bag, pulled out a half-eaten package of sunflower seeds, and handed it to him. "Thanks for your help around the plate today."

His chubby face split into a grin. "Certainly, Mr. Cooper."

I pack up the rest of my equipment and again think about the team we'll have next year. Breaking my future-thinking, Lefty Oliver sat just a couple guys down to my right. He was sliding on his usual boots.

"Fridge?" he asked while pointing toward Billy who threw a heaping handful of seeds in his mouth. "What did your biggest fan say to ya?"

Feeling certain Billy hadn't mentioned Lefty's name during the inquiry, I made light of the question saying, "Some amateur salesman wants to talk."

I thought it was another scout trying to recruit me or Bo—probably for a small-time program where the chance of getting noticed for the elite level would be next to impossible. Even if you play great at a place like that, you get chalked up as a has-been (and never-will-be), especially for a catcher like me. A catcher's career is short-lived due to the physical abuse it puts on one's body.

But I was thankful for being noticed. I slipped out the side of the dugout and saw Bo, our junior all-Tri-County shortstop, engaged in conversation with a tall man. This sharp dressed man was wearing a blazer and trousers that could only be fitted by a tailor. As for his hair, definitely salon styled. Hell, maybe even blow-dried. As I approached them both, this city slicker scout was already extending his hand and greeting me. "Ricky Cooper, it's a pleasure. Great game, kid."

"Great game?" I thought. "We just took it on the chin." I thanked him anyway.

He maintained his hold on my hand with the same firm grip. "That was quite a shot in the top of the fifth, and Bo here tells me it set a school record."

"Yes sir," I replied.

"And your work behind the plate is just what we're looking for. Boys, I'm on a tight schedule. Here is a great opportunity for the both of you." He handed us each a business card. His last words were: "Boys, do us all a favor and be sure to call the number on the card." And he walked away.

Puzzled, I waited till he was out of hearing distance, turned to Bo, and asked, "Who the hell was that?"

Bo shrugged his shoulders. "Don't know, Fridge."

As we looked down at the cards simultaneously, we both read, "Harry Slicker Services, Serving All Your Service Needs."

Still puzzled, I slid the card into the back pocket of my dusty uniform pants. "Bo, that was pretty odd. Well, see you on the flip." It was time to go. Besides, Deva Diamond, Bo's girlfriend, was walking toward us. With a fist bump and a quick, "I can't wait till next year," I headed back into the dugout.

Bo replied, "Me too, Fridge."

Deva Diamond was Beaver Falls High's Miss Priss. I swear she thinks she walks on red carpet everywhere she goes. As I walked past her, I acted like the gentleman my mother raised me to be. "Have a nice summer, Deva."

"Go to hell, Ricky!" She never missed a step on that never-ending red carpet.

I didn't expect anything else from the bitter princess. She was the only child of a prom-queen mom and a dad she never met. Deva believed there were far better things outside of Crossroad County, and she had Bo locked up to help pave her way with certainty.

Upon reentering the dugout, I heard Coach Gibbs giving orders. "Hurry it up, boys. Red, at least wait to get on the damn bus before taking the jock strap off. Billy…where the hell is Billy?"

"Right here, Grandpa," Billy said sheepishly.

"Go tell Gus to fire up the bus and point it toward Crossroad County."

As we approached the bus, we were welcomed by an ovation of family, friends, and Beaver baseball fans. Thankfully they didn't overdo it. Other than a few tears welling up in the corners of some of the mothers' eyes or dripping from J. J.'s little sister's jawline, for the most part everyone held it together.

"Nothing to be ashamed of boys." said Mr. Junker. Mrs. Junker was pulling each of us one by one into her surgically enhanced chest.

"We'll get 'em next year, boys," Bucky's grandpa shouted.

"Congrats, Fridge, on the big swat record," said Big Red's dad.

I finally got through the crowd to my parents. Mom wasted no time throwing her arms around me. With wet eyes and a muffled voice, she told me how proud she was of me.

"Hey, Dad."

"Hey, Son...Ricky?"

"Yes, Dad?"

"That might have been one of the finest pitching performances I've seen at the high school level in quite some time, other than the changeup he threw you in the fifth. Way to stay back on the ball and then shift into your release."

"Just like you've taught me, Dad."

"You're a great student of the game, Son."

"All aboard," said Gus, our bus driver, while standing on the last step and waving his Beaver ball cap.

"Here, Ricky. I packed you some peanut butter and banana sandwiches for the ride home," said Mom.

Grabbing my stomach, I told her, "You're the best." Then I turned to Dad and did our father-son, four-step handshake. It ends with us blowing the smoke from our index-finger pistols and then sliding them back into our holsters.

"Well, you better get saddled up on this yellow train, Son, before it leaves the station."

"Right on," I replied. "I'll see you guys at home."

"Are you taking Red home from the school?" Mom asked.

"Yes," I said.

Dad looked over my shoulder and said, "Maybe."

I turned to look. Sure enough, Big Red had himself buried in Mrs. Junker's mounds of joy for a second time.

"Classic Red," said Dad.

As we left Tournament Field, I stared out the back window of the bus. I said to myself, "At the end of next season, the fire that burns in my chest will only be quenched when I have a silver trophy in my hand as we parade it back to Crossroad County and down through the streets of Beaver Falls."

My vision of certainty was broken by a sunflower seed buzzing by my ear and smacking the window in front of me. Turning to find the culprit, I saw Red sitting across from me in his jersey and boxers pretending as though he were fast asleep. I reached in the sack of sandwiches Mom had packed, pulled one out, took aim at the brim of Red's ball cap, and fired.

"Holy smokes, Fridge! Have you gone mad?" I heard from a surprised Red after connecting.

I laughed as I said, "There. Peanut butter and banana." Looking down at the sandwich that now rested between his legs, he joined in the laughter.

We had about a one-and-a-half-hour ride back home. A lot of the team looked out the windows at the city, imagining what it would be like to live there. Me? I couldn't wait to get off the four-lane roads and back to country life, where the hills rolled and the air didn't smell like an exhaust pipe. Or maybe it was the fumes coming from Red's jock strap dangling from the back hatch for anyone following the bus to see. Red and I wolfed down a couple of sandwiches and were soon resting our tired eyes.

I awoke to Coach Gibbs demanding attention from the front of the bus. I knew we were getting back into familiar terrain by the ups and downs, twists and turns. "Listen up, boys. I'm not going to beat around the bush about how our season ended. In baseball, you have two teams, and after the final out, you either have more runs scored than your opponent or you don't. It doesn't matter if it's the first game of the season or in the Tri-County semifinal. That's baseball. Besides, you have the rest of your lives to find out that life in general sometimes grants you the short end of the stick. So prepare yourselves for the unexpected." Coach Gibbs half raised his arm and paused for a second studying his mangled right hand.

"Anyways, we have most of this team coming back next season. For you two seniors, this is the end of high school ball for ya. As for the rest of you, just because this season is in the books does not mean your bat and glove never come out of your equipment bag till next season. I'm already making Ricky and Bo joint captains for next season. They will be in charge of making sure you guys are keeping your arms in shape, getting some fielding practice, and getting a respectful number of cuts in. As most of you know, league rules prohibit me or any other paid coach to organize such activities. So the captains will report back to me periodically on your commitment to next season's team. Do I make myself clear?"

"Yes, Coach," we all said in cadence.

"Now, one more announcement: our awards banquet will be held this Saturday at the Irish Schnitzel. The dress is casual—but no ball caps. I want you guys to be on your best behavior and be sure to thank Red's parents for their hospitality." Coach finished his orders and sat back down just as Gus drove the bus onto our school's street.

Red said to J. J. (loud enough for the back half of the bus to hear), "Your mom can wear that same revealing casual top she had on today."

J. J. was sitting with his back to us. He didn't miss a beat. He extended his long arm up and left the longest finger of the five up alone. Now everyone laughed,

I thought to myself, "What a team."

Dropping Red off at his residence usually involves us chowing down some Irish-German food, because he and his parents live atop the finest restaurant in Crossroad County. Sitting on the south side of Beaver Falls, the Irish Schnitzel is a landmark for passersby and a staple for locals.

"You coming in, Fridge?" asked Red.

"What kind of question is that?" I replied.

"Well, I wasn't sure—with the loss and all."

"Since when did you start caring about anyone's feelings?"

"You're right, Fridge, but do you think I could at least get a hug good-bye?"

"Save it for Mrs. Junker." I laughed. "I'll race you in."

For a big boy, Red moves with surprising speed. He got to the entrance of the restaurant before me. He opened it with a bow. "Right this way, *Mrs. Junker.*"

Mr. McStein bellowed out from a stool at the bar, "The boys are back in town!" Half-loaded, he came over to us, threw an arm over both our shoulders, and paraded us around the horseshoe bar.

Most of the locals already knew our accomplishments over the few years of high school ball, but Mr. McStein was always sure to remind them. The passersby, on the other hand, were being formally introduced to arguably the best catcher/first baseman tandem in the history of Beaver High baseball. We heard a lot of, "Really?" and "It's a pleasure to meet two young men of your caliber," often followed by (mostly from the women), "I have a daughter about your age."

My response was always, "Thank you."

"I'll go get paper and a pen," said Red, eager as always.

We finally sat down and ordered the special. As we finished our veal spätzle, which was lightly covered with brown mushroom gravy, Red looked up at me. "Hey, Fridge, how come you think when my dad always introduces us as the best tandem he always starts with you?"

Savoring my last bite and taking my time swallowing, I looked at Red sincerely and asked him, "Do you need a hug?" I thanked the McSteins for their always-complimentary meal and told Red I would see him at the morning workout. I was off and headed to my home, where my parents were waiting for their son's return.

I lived less than a five-minute drive from the Schnitzel. I headed northeast and passed Dad's barbershop. As always, no matter what time day or night, I beeped the horn out of habit.

Or maybe it's out of acknowledgement of my childhood. I thought of the many good times we had as a family, spending the first ten years there and living only a few blocks from Red's. We had moved just outside town to a brick ranch house that sat on a couple of acres. It was nothing fancy, about what you'd expect on a barber and a schoolteacher's salaries, but it had enough elbow room for Dad and I to play some catch. It sure beat the park across from our old hacienda, where anyone who lived in that part of town would walk their dogs. The dog owners tended to forget to disarm the "land mines" their pets left behind; those land mines always seemed to be reclaimed by people who didn't own dogs themselves.

After the short drive, I saw the den light was still on. The blinds were open just enough for me to see the silhouettes of Mom and Dad in their recliners. As I walked in the house, I saw the sense of relief pouring from my parents. Being an only child has its perks, but it makes the parents a little overprotective at times.

"Hi, Ricky," Mom said.

"Son?"

"Yes, Dad?"

"I shouldn't have to remind you that if you're going to be a little late to call and let us know."

"Yeah, about that…"

Mom looked up from her book. She was waiting for a well-planned excuse.

"Mom, do you have to look at me like that?"

"Just waiting to hear the reason, Ricky. That's all."

I recite the cause for my late arrival. "Well, I thought it would be just a quick bite of delicious special and out the door, but Mr. McStein was into the stouts when we got there and wanted to show us off around the bar. And well…you know…tell everyone about the dynamic duo who were blessing them with their presence. Finally, Mrs. McStein came to our rescue."

Mrs. McStein had literally pried the two celebrities out from under the shoulders of the not-so-surefooted German debater. We finally got to sit down and eat, interrupted by periodic congratulatory remarks about the season that we helped put together for Beaver Falls High.

Mom looked over at Dad with a smile and said, "Well, Dad, what you think of this explanation?" All Dad could do was start laughing. All Mom could do was shake her head.

"Listen guys, it's a little later than I thought. Next time, I'll make the call."

That helped relieve Mom's worries. "Ok, Ricky. Thank you."

I made my way to the stairs, "Hey, Son?" Dad said. I stopped and looked back. "You wanna talk about the game?"

"No. Like always, I'll wait till tomorrow."

"Absolutely, Son."

As I almost reached the stairs, Dad called to me again. "Son?"

"Yes, Dad?"

"You just finished up your junior year of high school, and there are many colleges recruiting your talents. They're looking not only on the diamond but in the classroom as well. Shortly we're gonna have to sit down and at least start to eliminate some of the options— start narrowing down what is best for you on and off the playing field."

"Sure thing, Dad, but right now I have to go put a workout plan together for me and some of the boys for the morning."

"Aren't you gonna take just a few days off? It's been such a long season, Ricky," Mom said.

"Oh, I forgot to mention to you guys: Coach named Bo and me joint captains for next year already."

Dad choked on the sip of ale he had just taken. He cleared his throat.

Mom gasped, "Are you all right, Hon?"

He spit out in a convincing voice, "Bo, a captain? Don't get me wrong, he has a very bright future in the game, but his leadership ability is nonexistent. Bo is all about Bo, and that Deva girl won't let him forget it. Let me ask you this, Son: you said you and some of the guys are working out in the morning, right?"

"Yes."

"Ok, now is Bo one of those guys?"

"No."

"Exactly my point."

I shrugged my shoulders and headed upstairs. "Good night."

I could still hear Dad muttering about Bo. "What the hell is Gibbs thinking, giving that kind of leadership role to a kid who thinks of nothing but himself and maybe that Diamond girl?"

I smiled a bit at Dad's rant. Once in my room, I shut the door, threw my bat bag in the corner, and collapsed onto the king-sized mattress. I was still trying to swallow the Tri-County semifinal loss.

2

Sometimes in life, you have to look back and remember the times when parents, coaches, or elders in general told you something that you brushed off as though you had nothing to worry about. Well, giving credit to my dad's thoughts about Bo, our returning all Tri-County shortstop didn't waste any time calling Harry Slicker Services. It turns out Harry Stroker was trying to recruit Bo and me off the Beaver Falls baseball team and onto the reigning Tri-County champs, the hated Easton Prep Sluggers.

Honestly, I forgot about meeting the snake that day—until Mom, a couple days later, demanded I get out my bat bag. She needed to wash my uniform. Mom came out of the laundry room holding a business card in her hand. "Who is Harry Slicker?" she asked.

"He wanted to talk to Bo and me, but he never really said why. He handed us each a business card and said we should do ourselves a favor and call the number on it."

Dad was reading the newspaper nearby. He lowered the paper just enough for his eyes to clear the top and said, "That's odd."

"Ya, I kinda thought the same thing," I replied.

"Son?" Dad asked, "What did this Harry look like?"

"A greased-up banker."

"A businessman?"

"Yes."

Dad squinted. "A scout? Bring me that card," he said as he motioned to Mom. "They never dress like a broker. They usually have an insignia of some sort on a ball cap or shirt they're wearing that shows what program they're from."

After Mom handed Dad the card, he read it out loud. "Harry Slicker Services, serving all your service needs." He looked up. "Who the hell is Harry Slicker?"

"Well, find out by calling the number," said Mom.

Dad wasted no time. He picked up the phone and dialed the 1-800 number. "Yes, I'll hold." He looked over at me and said, "I don't have a good feeling about this—Yes, this is Mr. Cooper..." The next five minutes only added to my realization that you aren't gonna buffalo my dad. It doesn't matter how pretty you want to paint a picture, because he looks at it from the frame in.

"Listen, Hairy Dicker. Never approach my son again!" He slammed the phone down and addressed me seriously. "Son, the older you get, the more you're gonna realize there are more horse's asses out there than there are horses. Harry Slicker is one of them."

"So what did he want with me?" I asked.

"Well, it turns out that Hairy Shitter was wrangled to recruit you and Bo to go and play for Easton Prep."

"Really?" I asked with disgust.

"Really," Dad said.

"Why wouldn't they send someone from Prep to come and recruit?"

"Because it's against Tri-County rules."

"But they can have someone else try?"

"No, that's against the rules too, but it makes it a lot easier to get away with."

"Huh. Well, no worries here," I assured him.

"Not so fast, Son, sounds like Hairy Lipper has ol' Bo talked into becoming a Prep slugger."

. . .

As it turned out, Bo and Diamond Digger Deva eventually moved fifty miles east to an apartment a block from Easton Prep. Supposedly, Deva made enough money working day shifts at a tanning salon to afford the apartment. I just wish I had the chance to talk to Bo before he made his decision, but I'm sure my input would have been trumped anyway.

Knowing we had to find a shortstop, I drove to Coach Gibbs's house to see if he was aware of the situation. As I approached Coach's house, I was glad to see he was on his garden tractor mowing his front lawn. I parked my truck in his driveway, got out, flipped the tailgate down, and took a seat. I saw he was almost done.

Watching Coach mowing in his bib overalls, the sun kept off his head and shoulders by his wide-brimmed straw hat, I couldn't help but think, "How could a guy once blessed with so much talent end up like this?" Not that I didn't respect Coach or anything. He was a teacher, coach, and farmer John. It's just that at one time, he was sought by recruiters for the highest level of baseball.

I was brought back from my stereotyping by the sound of the mower deck being disengaged and the throttle being slowly backed off to idle. Then Coach turned the motor off. I jumped off the tailgate and slammed it shut. Coach Gibbs waved me over to the back deck of his home.

"Hey, Coach. Sure is a nice place you got here."

"Yes, Ricky. Martha and I enjoy our time here."

Looking out at the pond in the backyard I asked him, "There any fish in it?"

"Many kinds."

"I didn't know you fished, Coach."

He smirked a bit, took another pull on his cigarette, and said, "There are a few things you don't know about me, Ricky."

Not knowing really what to say to that, I quickly got to the reason for my visit. "Coach, the reason why I—"

"I already know about Bo, Ricky." He paused for another draw and then blew out the smoke. "It's a shame he jumped ship on us. I'm sure they painted a pretty picture for him."

Looking out at the pond I said, "Yeah, they probably did."

"What about you, Ricky?" Coach asked. "Are they painting the same picture for you?"

"They tried," I said. "But, Coach, my picture is here with Beaver Falls baseball. I started drawing this picture when I was five, and you better believe I intend to finish painting it here."

He butted his cigarette and exhaled. "Ricky Cooper, you never cease to amaze me. Here we are losing our starting shortstop to Easton Prep, whose team clearly now will repeat—yet again—as the Tri-County tournament winner next season. And yet, here you are, still determined to…" Coach stopped in the middle of his sentence.

He was gazing out over his backyard as it came to him. "I have an idea. If Prep wants to play hardball, then we're gonna throw a curve ball right back at 'em. Besides, I still have the best all-around player on my team."

I was shocked by what Coach just said, because he doesn't toot on anyone's horn. I mean, just a few days before, I had broken the Beavers' all-time record for home runs, and all I got was a simple nod from him as I rounded third. Even during the season after a team win, he soberly and casually stated, "Congratulations on doing your job."

"Coach, I'm a little confused here. What do you mean by throwing a curve ball back at them?

He lit up another smoke. "Let me show you some of these fish, and I'll explain."

■ ■ ■

As I left Coach Gibbs's place, I couldn't wait to get to the Irish Schnitzel to tell Big Red what was going on. Also, I wanted to see what the dinner special was that night. When I opened the door to the restaurant, I saw Red standing behind the bar and washing some mugs. He greeted me with a question: "Did you hear about Bo?"

"Sure did."

"You don't look too disappointed, Fridge."

"Well," I said," at least we don't have to put up with Deva Diamond anymore."

"That's a good way to look at it."

"Listen, Red, I have an idea, but it involves you. Tell your parents you're going to need tomorrow evening off."

"I can make that happen," said Red, as he toweled off a mug.

"Good."

"So what's your idea?" Red asked.

"I'll tell you about it tomorrow evening, but for now, *dish boy*, I'll have the special."

"Coming right up, *ma'am*."

After I wiped the bowl of Irish stew clean with a piece of pumpernickel bread, I told Red, "Be at my house by five o'clock tomorrow evening. Wear a pair of gym shorts and a t-shirt. Oh! And be sure to bring your baseball equipment."

Red was busy but gave me a quick thumbs-up.

On my way out, I poked my head into the kitchen and told Mrs. McStein, "The stew was delicious, as always. Thanks again."

"Anything for you, Ricky."

That night, I went home and filled my parents in on Coach's idea. They were all in. Now, all I had to do was just pull it off.

■ ■ ■

As I waited for Red, I recited some phrases I thought would convince a father I'd never met to allow his son to come play baseball for the Beavers. I heard a muscle car's gears shift and knew Red would be pulling into the driveway any second. I was already in my truck.

He pulled up alongside me and said, "I'll drive."

"It would be best for me to drive."

He revved up his motor. "Why?"

"Because we're going to south Crossroad County."

Red looked shocked. "You mean milk yankers' country?"

"Yep."

"Yeah, you can drive," Red said. "Besides, I just gave ol' Ruby here a wash and wax. I don't need any horse droppings up under the fenders."

"Cool," I said. "Jump in. We gotta roll."

After we listened to a couple of our favorite country songs, Red said, "Fridge, why the hell are we going to south Crossroad and taking our ball gloves with us?"

"All right," I said. "Here's the scoop. Bo is gone, so we need a shortstop. I went over to Coach's house yesterday, and we talked about the situation. Believe it or not, Red, Coach actually showed some emotion: he was pissed off."

"Really?"

"Really. But here's the good part: Coach isn't gonna sit back and let Prep get away with it without putting up a fight."

"Coach said 'fight'?" asked Red.

"No," I replied. "He said 'throw a curve ball back at them.'"

"Ok, then what's the curve?" Red asked.

"All right. Coach and his wife like to take drives down through Amish country."

"That explains why his truck smells like a horse stall."

"Let me finish," I said. "So supposedly there's this little Amish stand down on Township Road 10. Coach and his wife frequently drive to it for the fruits and vegetables. Well, once while Martha was taking her time picking out the produce, Coach sat in his truck and watched this father and son playing catch on a makeshift ball field across the street. Red, you know how hard it is to get a compliment out of Coach."

"Virtually impossible," said Red.

"Well, he said that the Amish boy had a golden glove, a strong accurate arm, and could drive the ball foul post to foul post or anywhere in between. He said if we could land him on the team, our infield would be lights out with a solid outfield. Inserting this kid into our lineup is gonna make the opposition have a tough time keeping us from rounding the bases."

"You're talking about Coach Gibbs saying this? Right?" asked Red.

"I know it's not his normal self, but this whole situation seemed to spark a fire in him."

"Was he drinking?" asked Red.

"No, but he was chain-smoking cigarettes," I said.

Red choked on his sports drink. "Coach is a chain smoker?"

"One right after another," I said. "Keep that between us."

"No sweat, Fridge. You know me. Besides, Coach just keeps getting cooler by the second."

"All right," I said. "This is Township Road 10, and I believe right up there is the produce stand."

"So what's our plan?" asked Red.

"Just follow my lead."

"Can I at least hold your hand?" asked Red fluttering his eyelashes.

"Not this time, Deva."

We pulled into the lot of the produce stand and parked facing the empty makeshift ball field. Red said, "Maybe they're still milking or pitching manure." As I got out of my truck, he asked, "Where're you going?"

"To get some fruit. I'm starving."

"Wait."

I paused and looked back. "What?"

"I need your hand," said Red, as he flipped his hair.

I grabbed some apples and peaches. Red said, "Hey, Fridge, I didn't know the Amish could grow melons this big." We both looked over at the Amish girl who was running the stand. She looked at Red with a little smile and giggled. Red and I have been best friends since we were five years old, and this was the first time I've ever seen his cheeks blush. I quickly looked back down at the fruit I had as though I hadn't seen Red's reaction toward the girl.

As I was paying for my fruit, Red set two melons on the counter and said, "I'll take your melons, too." He quickly tried to rephrase it by saying, "I'll have your melons." He was getting a little worked up. He put his hands on the melons on the counter and said, "These. I'll take these melons."

I headed to the truck, laughing. Red said, "What the hell is so funny, Fridge?" as he carried two large melons out to the truck.

"Oh, nothing, Red. I just can't get over the size of the produce here."

Red glared at me. "Not a word to anyone, Fridge, about what just happened."

"No sweat, Red. You know me."

We realized we could hear the distinctive sound of a bat on a ball some distance away. After grabbing our gloves and a couple of apples from the produce sack, we met in front of the truck. "How're you gonna pull this one off, Fridge?"

"Just follow my lead."

"Always, Fridge."

"Hello there!" I called out to the father and son out on the makeshift playing field. I assumed the man who turned to face us with a ball and bat in his hand was Mr. Kuber, the father of the ballplayer Coach had told me I should meet. Red and I waved at the duo and crossed Township Road 10.

"You sure about this?" Red said under his breath.

I wasn't sure, so I didn't answer his question directly. "Just get ready to field some catches at first. Hello!" I said again. "My buddy and I saw you playing some ball while we were buying some fruit." The Amish man glanced back across the road. A moment of silence filled the air until I extended my hand and said, "Sir, my name is Ricky Cooper, and this here is Red McStein. We love to practice the game of baseball any chance we can."

Shaking my hand, the gentleman says, "The name is Kuber."

"Well, it's a pleasure, sir."

The Amish boy who had been taking fielding practice was beating a pocket into his mitt as he waited on the next ground ball. From the shortstop position he asked his father, "What do they want?"

"To practice with us," the father answered.

"Let them play," the shortstop hollered back.

"Ok," Mr. Kuber said. "It would be good for Jonas to practice on some throws over to you wearing the first baseman's mitt," he told Red. Without hesitation, Red slid on his glove and took off for first.

I spoke up. "I'll shag for you here at the plate."

After a few ground balls and throws over to first and then back home, our plays became simple clockwork. Red glanced back at me. We both knew we had to get this Jonas on our team.

Mr. Kuber kept hitting grounders from home plate. After about a dozen plays of error-free baseball, Mr. Kuber asked, "Ricky Cooper, what do want with my Jonas?" "Sir," I answered, "we need a shortstop next season for the Beaver Falls High baseball team. With your permission and son's willingness to come and play, I believe we can win next year's Tri-County tournament.

Mr. Kuber paused in the middle of his swing and caught the ball. He looked directly at me and smiled. "I think Jonas would like that." He tossed the ball back up and sent another grounder into the gap. Jonas answered it with a backhand and a flick over to Red.

Amazed, I pointed to the machine wearing the glove, and asked, "He ever miss?"

"Wait till you see him hit."

We sealed the deal that early summer evening right there on the makeshift field. I explained what the requirements were for Jonas to become a student athlete at Beaver Falls High. The trickiest one was passing a ninth-grade-level acceptance test. Already ahead of the game, I explained that I had it worked out with my mom to help tutor Jonas over the summer to get him up to speed.

It was a little easier than I thought to get Jonas on our team, especially because he was the youngest of seven and was required to do so much work on the farm. But it almost seemed like Mr. Kuber thought he owed it to his family to give Jonas an opportunity outside the farm. I also kicked in the idea of Red and I helping out with the hay bailing throughout the summer and any other labor the family might need from young, energetic workers. Mr. Kuber liked the idea. He seemed pleased to point out Red was roughly the size of an ox.

Mr. Kuber then asked, "What about transportation and the twenty-minute country ride by vehicle to the school? It's about forty-five minutes with Elroy pulling Jonas in the buggy."

"I'll help transport as much as possible," I answered. "And there's the Oliver twins, who live up the hill on County Road 20. We'll work it out."

"Are you talking about Jon Oliver's boys?"

"Yes," I said, "Lefty and Righty."

Thinking for a second, Mr. Kuber said, "It would be no problem for Jonas to get to the Oliver farm with Elroy if they don't mind him parking and pasturing Elroy till Jonas returned."

Rolling the dice on the Olivers being on board with everything, I nodded my head in agreement. "Yeah, shouldn't be a problem."

Jonas was filled with excitement and anticipation. He asked his dad, "You think Mom is going to agree with this?"

Mr. Kuber answered with authority, "Jonas, you let me handle the telling of the situation to your mother. Besides we're getting good trade labor here."

As we left on our way to the Olivers' place, Big Red was still upset that I had volunteered some of his summer days for work on an Amish farm. "Fridge, do you really want to smell like a horse's rear for half of the summer?"

I told him, "If that's what it takes to get and keep Jonas on our team then, yes, I do. Besides, consider the labor as our workouts and maybe—just maybe, Red—we can get you some more Amish melons from across the road."

Red was a little disgusted. He looked out the side window. "Go to hell, Fridge."

"All right, Big, but will you at least hold my hand?"

Getting the Olivers on board was, as Red would put it, "as easy as their oldest daughter." They agreed to allow Jonas to park his horse and buggy there and to give him a ride back and forth from school and baseball, which would save me a lot of mileage on the pickup truck.

That summer, Red and I held up our end of the bargain with the Kubers. Red would later admit to me he didn't mind smelling like a horse stall for half the summer, because he felt as strong as the horse pulling the wagon. I would have to agree with him. We had an endless supply of fresh milk, and we were fed some of the best homemade grub we could handle by Mrs. Kuber and one of Jonas's sisters. It just so happened that the sister I'm talking about was also the Amish girl who ran the family produce stand across the road. This was added motivation for ol' Big.

Throughout the summer, Mom tutored Jonas. He passed the school's entrance exam. Every chance we had, we were working on our game there on the makeshift ball field. A few times, I got most of the team down there for practice away from our Beaver Falls home field. Some of the guys liked it. Some of them thought it was too far out to play on a dirt infield, an outfield made up of scattered patches of grass, and the edges of the field marked off by a white picket fence. But we all loved the long picnic table full of chow the family made available at the end of practice.

■ ■ ■

So, now that you're caught up to speed, I need to explain how I'm going to deliver my senior season to you. You'll be standing beside me as though you're watching the start of the season and listening all the way to end of the book. I will ensure you of this on and off the field of play. Besides, live action is always the best way to deliver an amazing story. By now, you realize my sincerity. Let's enjoy the Pre-season together toward the quest for the Tri-County trophy.

3

"Thanks for picking me up, Fridge."

"Not a problem, Jonas."

"Here's a fresh quart of milk," he says while handing it to me.

Wasting no time, I twist the top off and chug the first half. Wiping the milk 'stache from my mouth, I say to Jonas, "Now that is udderly fantastic."

"Yep, got it right out of the teat this morning."

"Can't get any fresher than that."

Waving at Mr. Kuber while I pull out of the drive and onto Township Road 10, I ask Jonas, "You have all your stuff, including your spikes?" He doesn't like to wear them while playing.

"Sure do, Fridge."

"Good." I down the last of the milk. "You'll need them for the scrimmage this evening." Sensing a bit of nervousness from our starting shortstop, I quickly speak up: "Don't worry about the game later, Jonas. With your natural ability it will be a simple walk in the park."

"Fridge, it's just that it's the first time that I'll be playing in front of fans."

I laugh. "Jonas, you just rely on your talent, relax, and have fun. Besides, it's just practice. The majority of fans won't show up till the games really start counting. By then you'll enjoy the buzz." He sits back in the passenger seat and his face relaxes a bit. With a little more influence, I say, "Jonas, if you start to feel like you are losing focus because of the butterflies circling your stomach, just look over at our first baseman, Red, and remember the picture he gave your sister."

Jonas isn't able to keep from laughing. "Absolutely!"

I turn up the radio, and we listen to some country. I tell Jonas how much I'm starting to like this southern part of Crossroad County.

"Ya, it's all right."

"What do you mean about it being just 'all right'?"

"Well, you know, Fridge, it's a lot of work keeping a farm going with all the chores seven days a week. It doesn't leave much time for anything else, and the girls around here I just don't fancy."

"Well, Jonas, you have time to play baseball."

"Yes, Fridge, only because of you and Red coming out to the farm last summer on the recruitment trip and the labor trade you promised my dad. Honestly, I just don't see myself harnessing horses for the rest of my life. I love the game as much as you do, and I'm really starting to like school and the classroom work. I'm getting a good sense of acceptance from most of the students."

"You sure are adjusting rather quickly," I say.

"What about Abby Oliver?" I ask. "Do you enjoy her too?"

He grins. "Maybe."

After a moment of silence, he asks how I knew about his secret crush. I point to my eyes with two of the fingers on my right hand and then point out. "By maintaining focus on my surroundings."

"Do you ever *not* study your surroundings, Fridge?"

I pause for a moment. "No, that's not how great catchers work."

We then drive past the Oliver ranch. "Do you want me to stop and see if Abby needs a ride since her brothers are at an auction?" I asked. This brought a blush and a grin.

"No. Besides there's no room for her to sit in here." he says.

I follow up by saying, "You might want to watch how you phrase that."

"What do mean?"

"Well some girls might take the *no room* comment to heart."

"Why."

"Girls, especially at this age, are very self- conscience about their figure and the space it might take up."

"Huh?"

"Yeah it's a quick way to lose a dinner date." I say.

I drive on, and we listen to the radio, not saying much after the comment I made to Jonas, until we approach the school. I roll down the window and yell out to Buzzy Weiser, "You should have stayed where you were the other night." I slow down and pull alongside Buzzy. "Told ya, Buzzy. You weren't gonna slip by your old man with that alcohol breath and those glassy eyes."

"Ok, Mom," he says, not looking our way.

"So, Three Bag, you need a lift?" I asked our third baseman.

"Could have used one fifteen minutes ago, Fridge," he says, still not looking at us.

"Well, I had to pick up Jonas this morning 'cause the Olivers are at a livestock auction."

"Jonas should have saddled up Elroy and ridden the donkey into school," says Buzzy, now glancing over at the Amish boy.

Jonas says something in German. Buzzy comes to a halt. "What the hell did the straw hat just say?"

"Just hop in the bed of the truck for the last couple of blocks." I tell Buzzy,

"All right," he says.

Just as he puts a hand on the bed of the pickup, I hit the accelerator and leave him standing there in the rearview mirror.

Jonas is not quite sure why I just did that. "Fridge, Buzzy already doesn't like me. Now he's gonna think I had a part in leaving him behind."

"You let me handle the hotheaded Buzzy, Jonas. Besides, he needs to be taught a lesson, not only by his father but also by his peers."

"What do you mean by his peers, Ricky?" asks Jonas.

Thinking for a second, I reply, "Jonas, has your dad ever told you the expression, 'Hey, Son, you've got your head in the clouds'?" He pauses while looking at Buzzy's fading reflection in the side mirror.

"No, Fridge, Dad's expressions usually bring on more work."

"What are some of the sayings he used to try and teach you a lesson?" I ask.

"All, I don't know, Fridge, you know my Pa isn't much for words."

"Come on. Think about it," I say again.

Pausing for a moment, he replies. "Dad does often tell me 'In order for it to be done right, you must grab Duce by the horns.'" (Duce is their biggest bull in the pasture).

"Exactly!" I say.

"Exactly?" Jonas responds as though asking a question.

"Yes," I say. "That's how your old man expresses his lesson on keeping your head out of the clouds."

"By grabbing Duce by the horns?" he asks.

"No, by making sure you're coherent in what you're doing. He's explaining to you that if you physically are going to try and wrap your fingers around the horns of that beast, you must be totally focused on the game plan you better have thought through or you're going to be in for the ride of your life."

Laughing he says, "Yes, you would."

"Anyways," I say. "Back to Buzzy's head in the clouds. Buzzy's decision to leave Gunner's bonfire the other night, after sipping on some clear grain, could have cost not only himself but the innocent vehicle he might have not seen until it was too late. It's one thing to be told this by your parents, but it sinks in a little deeper being told by someone around the same age."

Jonas looks somewhat puzzled by the topic. "You sure have been taught the rights and wrongs of life."

"I've been fortunate to have it taught to me at an early stage in life, but even if someone tries to teach you something, it doesn't do any good unless you accept it."

I pull into the parking lot of the school and park next to "Ruby," with Big Red leaning on her hood. A few of Beaver Falls' finest dames are giggling and reminiscing with Red the stud. I get out of my old pickup, and three flirts serenade me in unison: "Hi, Ricky."

"Hello girls," I say, not paying too much attention to the chorus, which responds with a short giggle.

"Hey, Fridge," says Red. "What's with you picking up Jonas this morning?"

"The Olivers went to a livestock auction this morning," I tell him.

"Oh. Well, they should have taken Jonas with them. He knows more than they do about things that stand on four legs."

Jonas is still on the opposite side of the truck. "Hey, Red?" he starts, "next time I go pick out some chickens, I'll have you come with me—because of your knowledge of things that stand on two legs."

"I do know a lot about legs. Isn't that right, ladies?" Red fires back. The three girls turn and walk away.

"He's such a pig," says one of them.

Just then, J. J. Junker pulls up in a shiny, newer, full-size truck with our relief pitcher, Gunner Thompson, riding shotgun. "Top of the morning to you, gentlemen," says Gunner as he slams shut the passenger door. "You boys ready to kick some schoolgirl tail later?"

"Hell, ya!" says Red. "Who the hell we playing?"

"Fox Lake," I say.

"The Trappers?" asks Red.

J. J. now engages in the conversation. "Why would coach schedule a scrimmage against one of our season rivals?"

"Because I told him to," I say.

J. J. and the rest seem a little shocked, as if they want me to tell them a good reason why. I swing my bat bag over my shoulder. "Because I want to beat these fur traders twice this season."

"Oh! Hell, ya! Good call, Fridge!" Red's voice goes up in volume and pitch.

Walking up and into the school, I give a fist bump to Big. "I'll see ya third period for some weight training." I look over my shoulder and say the same to J. J. and Gunner.

As we make our way down the hall, Jonas says to me, "Fridge, when do you think I'll be able to lift weights during school hours with the team?"

"Well, Jonas, you've already done more lifting this morning on the farm than a lot of our guys get done during that hour of training with iron. Also, you need the extra hour during school for the study help in the library with Miss Oliver."

Smiling, Jonas agrees and says, "She sure does help make learning fun."

"You mean she persuades you with benefits that help lead you through those obstacles between you and the horizon of higher learning?"

"Yeah, I think so," he says.

Patting him on the back, I tell him, "Keep up the good work."

I hear Mr. Wood, the school's shop teacher, say, "Good luck this evening, Ricky," as he stands in his classroom doorway.

"Thanks, Mr. Wood."

After a few more steps, I hear, "Beat Fox Lake, Beavers!"

I look across the hall to see one of Beaver Falls' track team stars, Shot Put Dan, opening his locker. I tell Jonas to hold up a second. I make my way over to the county record holder for shot put throwing distance. "Hey, Meat, have you seen Motor Williams yet?"

"Ya, Fridge. I passed him on County Road 12 on the way in this morning. I slowed up the van and asked if he wanted a ride, and well...you know, Fridge, he looked over at me through the passenger window, smiled, and said, 'No thanks, Meat, I got this.' And there he went into sprint mode as though he wanted to race me in the van again."

"Typical," I say.

"Sure is."

"Well, if you happen to see him before third period, tell him that instead of going over to the track for yet another run, he should come to the weight room. And tell him to bring his equipment bag."

"Ya, sure thing, Fridge."

"Thanks," I turn to walk away, then stop and turn back. "Meat?"

"Ya?"

"Can I get one of those protein bars?" pointing at them atop of his locker.

"No problem, Fridge. Here are two," he says. I walk down the rest of the hallway with Jonas, devouring thirty grams of protein.

"Fridge, this scrimmage sounds more important than what you led me to believe earlier," says Jonas.

"Jonas, for me, every time I take the field, it's important—game, scrimmage, or even practice. You know this. But yes, you're right. It does seem like the buzz of Beaver baseball has already started," I say with a smile. Seeing Jonas tensing again, I throw my arm across his shoulders. "Just relax out there later and remember Red's photo." I push Jonas off toward the door of his first-period class and am once again surprised by how hard it is to move the sixteen-year-old's steel frame. I head to my prep-level physics class to ace the exam that's trying to test my knowledge on the subject.

TIMEOUT

Here's my school schedule, so we can keep things in order.

First period, I have physics. It's a great class to start the day. If you can accept its difficult theories, this mind-powering class is a necessity for a higher-level curriculum.

Second period, I have language arts. This class comes natural to me, thanks my in-home tutor for reading and writing. Thanks again, Mom.

Third period is weight training. This is one of Beaver Falls High's administration's best ideas. Not only do you get to work out during school hours, but it's also a credited class, which can help keep some of our slower-learning athletes eligible for competition.

Fourth period is lunch, my favorite. – Need I say more?

Fifth period is foreign language. *¡Buenos dias, amigo!*

Sixth period is calculus. This is my weakest link. In fact, I just recently asked the smartest girl in class if she could help improve my understanding of the confusing formulas.

Seventh period is study hall. Ok, I used to take this period as a teacher's aide for Mrs. Cooper, because she had a planning period at that time of the day that left her with an empty classroom. Her room is down the left wing of the school in the elementary building. But now I spend seventh period in the high school library with Miss Calculus.

TIME IN

With the second period bell sounding and ending my Language Arts class, I get to go throw some weights around. On the way, I swing into the principal's office and ask Mrs. Willcall, the school secretary, "Could I ask Mr. Paddler a quick question?"

Before she can answer, I see Mr. Paddler, our school chief, lean back in his office chair and look out his door. "Ricky, my man, come on in," he says.

"Cool," I say and take a couple steps into his office.

"Have a seat, Ricky. What can I do for you?"

"I'm heading to the weight room for class, but I wanted to know if I could get your permission to allow Motor Williams and Bucky to go out from the weight room to the baseball field and get some much-needed batting practice."

"Sure, Ricky, I don't see a problem with that," he says.

"All right, then," I say, getting up to leave.

"Ricky, if there's anything else you see fit to do to bring back the Tri-County trophy, then have at it. I trust your judgment enough that you don't have to clear it with me first."

"Thanks, Mr. Paddler, I'll keep that in mind." A firm handshake solidifies the deal, and I am off to get stronger.

Walking down the hall from the office and through the lobby, I have to stop and admire myself through the glass of Beaver Falls High's athletes' achievement awards case. I hold a few records, but my proudest to date is the home run record that I set last season.

"All right, all right," I hear, and feel a hand on my shoulder. "Yes, that's you in there. Now come on, princess. Let's go see if we can get your head any bigger."

I see Red's reflection in the glass. "Look," pointing at the reflection, "If you don't pick it up this year, your limited achievements will keep you on this side of the glass instead of holding records from the inside."

Red sighs. "Are you ready or what, Mr. Record Holder?"

"I was born ready, Mr. Pageant Judge."

As I walk into the locker room, I see Motor Williams must have gotten the message from Shot Put Meat and has his equipment bag with him.

Seeing me, Motor comes over and says, "Ricky, what's up with me bringing my baseball bag to this class, man? It's cutting into my track time, bro."

"Motor," I say, "I've known you for a lot of years now, but this is the first year since middle school that you've taken up baseball again. Back in the day, when we played together, you were always the fastest on the team."

"Still am," he says.

"Yes you are. Also, you could cut down a fly ball that most out-fielders could only dream of getting leather on."

"Still can." He nods.

"Yes," I say, "but, Motor, let's face it. You hit like shit."

A little shocked by the knock of his stick, he grins and says, "Ya, man, you've got a point there. But I can still lay down a bunt with the best of 'em."

I laugh and throw my arm across his slim shoulders. I tell him about the plan I conjured up for him and Bucky. So, after a change of clothes, Bucky and Motor head out to the field, hopefully to groove a better swing. The rest of us slap chalk between our hands for a better grip on some barbells, and with a playlist full of madness blaring, it is time to rock and roll.

During the sixty-minute regimen, Big Red McStein is in one of his no-holds-barred attitudes. It's partly to do with my little comment while we were standing in front of the trophy case in the lobby, and also with the fact that weight training is the only class Red gets an "A" in. As Red's best friend, I'm really the only one who's allowed to talk to him while he's in his element of destruction in the weight room.

Already holding the class record for the bench, Red is only ten pounds shy of holding the squat record, which is currently held by Shot Put Dan. Feeling my spot partner's adrenaline in the air, I know there is about to be a showdown on the squat rack.

After doing his last set of shoulder presses, Red wordlessly gives me the nod to book the contest. Looking back at him I say, "All right, Big, I'll get it set up." I walk over to the incline bench, where Shot Put Dan is standing behind his partner as a spotter. I tap him on the shoulder and make him aware of his challenger.

He looks across the gym at Red. "About damn time!" Knowing Dan's comment is only going to fuel Red's raging fire, I realize the odds of the record falling are now in favor of Big Red. I whistle for everyone's attention. "Listen up." The sounds of bars of steel being racked and dumbbells of iron being set down quiet the crowd as I gain total control of the floor...almost. "Gunner," I say.

"Ya, Fridge?"

"Turn Satan off," I say, pointing to the jam box. "Ok, Red here is feeling his oats this morning and wants to challenge Dan's squat record. Shot Put has accepted the invitation."

There were a couple cheers. "There's no way," someone added.

I raise my hand and again have silence. "So, since the bar is already set, Red goes first to try to tie Dan's record. If he succeeds, then Dan gets a shot at setting a new record. If Dan fails his attempt, then Red gets to try the higher amount of weight. Is everyone clear on the rules?" I ask.

"Ya, Fridge, let's get it on!"

"All right," I say, "load the bar."

Half the class is rooting for Shot Put Dan, and the other half is pulling for Big Red. I'm sure you know where my allegiance lies, but for now I'm in charge of both guys and making sure their squats are parallel and legal.

Hearing some of the guys place bets, the Irish-German walks into the squat rack, dips his head under the bar carrying the massive load, and sets the back of his shoulders against it. He lifts the bar off the rest and takes a half step back. The room is otherwise silent as Red squats down to parallel and back up to lock his knees. Nobody says a word until he racks the weight safely on the rests, and only then does the room get loud. As he exits the squat rack, Red is still stone-cold silent. He knows his mission is not over yet.

Now it is Meat's turn to try to set a new record. He instructs the guys to add ten more pounds. With the new record weight hanging from the bar, Meat positions it on his shoulders. The room again falls silent. As he clears the rests, the bar is bending from the forty-five-pound plates. Meat lowers until his thighs are parallel to the floor. He pauses for a moment, and it becomes clear that he can't straighten back up. He leans forward, allowing the safety bars to catch the record weight.

Now half the audience is excited that a new record might be set. The other half seems not so sure. It is Red's turn to try to fulfill his goal. It takes three guys to lift the bar full of weights back up to the rests, and Red wastes no time getting his shoulders back under the bar. The madman finally speaks: "This one is for all you doubters."

With a lift and half a step back to get in position, Big Red McStein gradually starts his descent—while simultaneously making the sharpest sound exit from his butt. The sound changes in pitch continuously as he crouches down to parallel. Everyone stands in awe of this spectacle of human effort. I think most of us aren't even thinking about the record squat he is delivering. As the weight starts to ascend, the symphonic hymn of music from Red's backside does not stop until the school squat record has a new owner, and possibly the Tri-County now has a new record for finest fart ever.

Amazed, no one says a word as Red safely sets the weight to rest. Not until Red turns to face the stunned crowd and bursts open in laughter does the weight room explode with the same. Now I've been laughing with Red for a long time, but this moment is off-the-chart classic Big Red. Most of the class is in actual pain in their stomachs from laughing. "Unbelievable!" someone says.

"Well done!" says someone else—for both accomplishments, I assume.

As Red is walking by me with his chest pushed up and out like a proud peacock, he bumps me with his elbow and says, "Put that in your trophy case!"

I'm still laughing. "Where are you going?" I ask.

"To the locker room. I think I just shit myself."

Soon after, as the chart buster and third period class was coming to an end, it's time for everyone's favorite time of the day: lunchtime. As I stand in the chow line, I hand Red two lunch trays. He looks at me and asks, "What are you doing?"

"Exactly what it looks like. We're getting two lunches today."

"All right, but you're buying my second one 'cause I only brought enough money for one and an extra chocolate milk."

"Yes, our second lunch is on Pringle."

"You mean, 'Cheddar'?" asks Red.

"Yes. After I told Shot Put Dan about you wanting to challenge his record, he was so ready to accept, he walked away from his spot partner and left Pringle in the middle of his set. So when I helped finish spotting him I wagered a little lunch bet."

"What if I didn't win the challenge?" Red asks.

"Well, that's why it's called a bet."

"Bullshit," Red says. "How did you know I was gonna set the record today?"

"Well, being aware of my best friend's controllable habits, I figured after the dinner we had last night at the Irish Schnitzel and the protein shake you were drinking this morning while sitting on Ruby's hood, we were all past due for a classic tune by Big Red McStein."

"You bet on my farting ability?" asks Red.

I laugh. "No, on the squat record."

Red is trying to move forward in the lunch line. He's also still looking at me. "No, Fridge, how did you know I was going to beat then set the record?"

I simply point to my eyes then out.

"Classic Fridge," says Red as he looks away.

We finally reach the start of the serving line. Mystery Monday's menu is revealed as a heaping scoop of Big Red's favorite school lunch: beans and wieners. After the delivery of protein that now lies on both lunch trays, he says, "Hell yeah! My gas tank is about on 'E.'"

With a raspy voice, the lunch lady says, "Here's a little extra, Mr. McStein. I know how much you like beans and wieners."

"Yes I do, Mrs. Ash, and be sure to tell your daughter, Virginia, I said hello."

Making our way down the counter, I say to Red as I'm grabbing two fruit cups, "Mrs. Ash's daughter is twenty years older than us. What are you doing telling her to tell Virginia you said hello?"

Pointing at his eyes Red says, "I'm staying aware of my surroundings. Let me tell ya, Fridge, that Virginia, although twenty years senior of us, is still a slim one."

Reaching the end of the line, I am happy to see the dessert for Mystery Monday is peanut butter squares topped with chocolate, Beaver Falls High School's most delicious dessert.

"Thank you, lunch queens," I say as I walk away from the cashier carrying two full lunches. Of course the chow hall has the typical tables, and walking through the room, I usually get glances from some student fans. Today's a different story.

"Trappers suck, Beavers rule!" I hear from the first table. They're speech team members. With a wink, I quickly get a thumbs-up from the bunch.

Walking past the next set of tables is always interesting. If you wear a jean jacket and have greasy hands from working on a truck or car, this is where you sit.

"It starts later, Fridge," I hear from Mustang Jones.

"Yes it does," I shoot back.

"No," he says, "What time's the game start later?"

"Oh...first pitch is five o'clock."

"Good," he says, "Sally and I will be there."

I think to myself, "That's interesting. I've never seen Mustang and his girlfriend, Sally, out at the baseball field." I say back to him, "Awesome, the more the merrier."

Next I hear Darryl Drummer say, "Hey, Fridge, you got a second?"

Stopping at the band table I said, "Ya, what's up, D.D.?"

"What do you think about some of us" as he looks down at the table then back at me "putting together a pep band for this evening's game?" he asks.

I'm a little stunned "Totally!"

"Great!" he exclaims with excitement and turns to another band member for a high five.

Walking away, I start to second-guess myself about what I told Jonas earlier about the size of the audience for this evening's scrimmage. "Let's just hope he remembers the calming effect of Big Red's picture gift to his sister," I think. I reach my usual spot and sit between Finn, our quiet second baseman, and Bucky. I can still hear students talking in anticipation about the game.

As Red walks through the aisles of tables, he also receives cheers for Beaver baseball. He makes his way to the letterman table and sits down across from me. "What the hell is going on around here? I mean, before this morning I didn't even know who the hell we were even playing tonight. Now, I almost feel like the idiot of the baseball team. Shit, even the freshman chess team said to checkmate the Trappers later, whatever the hell that means."

Bucky, our most politically correct player on the team speaks up: "Well, Red, you see, in chess you have to take your opponent's—"

Before Bucky can finish, Red cuts him off. "Bucky, shut the hell up. I know you have to take your opponent's queen in order to win chess. What do you think I am, an idiot?"

Grinning with a mouth full of teeth that looks like a hay rake jammed with half his lunch, Bucky says, "Actually, Red, in order to beat your opponent in the strategic game of chess, you must check and then mate the opponent's king."

Red pauses and gets an irritated look on his face. "Whatever, Bucky. All I know is I'd rather mate with the queen, not the king."

I change the subject. "Bucky, where the hell is Motor?"

Although his mouth is full, Bucky answers. "He'th at the twack getting hith run in."

"Does Motor ever stop running?" Red asks between bites.

"No," I say. "But it's what has given him the opportunity to run cross-country at the next level."

Once again, we start to hear shouts of, "Go get 'em, Beavers!" Someone hollers, "Stick a spork in 'em!" Gunner, J. J., and Buzzy all sit down at the table.

"Man," Gunner says, "these people are amped up for later. Hell, someone even said 'Stick a spork in 'em!'" he says as he holds up his eating utensil.

I finish one tray and set the second on top of it. "Well guys," I say, "looks like we're all gonna have to bring our 'A' game later."

"What about Lefty and Righty? They're gonna be there tonight, right?" asks J.J.

"Ya, they should be."

"What do you mean they should be?" asks Buzzy.

Before I can answer, Red looks down the table and says, "They're at an auction buying cows."

Buzzy doesn't hesitate. "Well, they should've taken Jonas with them," he says.

I get a sudden rush of adrenaline shooting through my body as I turn and look down at Buzzy. The brief silence is broken by Big Red saying, "Easy there, Fridge. Buzzy's only kidding." Red looks down the table. "Aren't ya, Buzzy?" he asks.

"Ya, Fridge, just joking around."

I know he is lying because of the way he treats Jonas off and on the field. When you're a catcher, every position faces you, and you face them. Great catchers know not only their own position, but every position on the field—and what it takes to play each. Now that Buzzy Weiser's buddy, Bo, is playing for Western Prep Sluggers, Buzzy can't take it that an Amish boy from deep Crossroad County can make the hardest plays look routine. What used to be base hits from a stretched-out third baseman and a diving shortstop are now being backhanded by a surefooted Jonas who's still able to turn and fire a shot to first base. On top of that, the boy can hit. Acceptance is Buzzy Weiser's own enemy, and he seems to have made good friends with jealousy.

"Well, if the Olivers aren't there later," says Gunner, "I'll start and finish the game, but I'm pegging a couple of them fur traders for sure."

"Good," says Red, "because I've got a few things for 'em when they reach my bag."

Bucky again tries to correct Red and says, "You mean first base."

"Ya," Red shoots back to him, "the one you rarely see."

Just then, Jonas arrives and wedges in between me and Bucky.

"What took you so long?" asks Red.

"Oh. Well, I wasn't quite sure about a problem in math class, so I stuck around a few minutes to have Mrs. Hagle show me the correct way of reaching the solution."

"You're taking this class work serious. That's the last teacher I'd give any more time than I had to," says Red.

"All hell, Red, she ain't so bad. Besides, I'd like to keep my B average going and just maybe by the end of the year I can make it to the "A" level."

"Geez," says Red, "if I didn't know any better, you almost sound like the guy sitting to your left."

All I can do is smile. As I finish the food on my second tray, some of the other students begin to walk by our table on their way out of the lunch hall. Quite a few of them are chanting, "Go, fight, win!" Daryl Drummer and some of his fellow marchers stop to tell us how excited they are for later.

As they walk away, Red says, "Excited for what?"

Drummer stops and turns to Red. "Fridge granted permission for our pep band to play at the game later."

"Since when have you horn blowers played for a baseball game?"

"That's easy," says Drummer. "The last time our alum played for you crotch arrangers was when Beaver Falls High had a leader like Fridge and a talented group of veteran players. And that team ended up bringing the Tri-County trophy back to our school."

"Well," says Red "can I make a few requests then?"

Drummer grins and says, "Sure, but let us work out some of the kinks first."

"Deal," says Red.

"Sure is nice to see everyone sharing in the excitement." This comes from Finn, a second baseman of few words.

"Yes, it is," I reply. "Guys," I say, "this evening, let's put together a performance that'll have our fellow classmates wanting more."

"What do ya mean, Fridge?" asks J. J.

"Well, tonight's game is on our own turf against a team that has been our school's cross county rivals since our grandfathers' playing days. Our fellow students dislike these fur nappers just as much as we do, so it's fun and exciting to see any of our school's sports programs not only win against them but beat 'em embarrassingly, especially on our own ground. So let's go out there later and give them what they are there for and more."

"What do you mean by 'more,' Fridge?" asks Jonas.

"Well, I want to keep this school spirit with us all season. I want them at every game. The bigger the better."

"Yes, bigger is better. Right, J. J.?"

"Piss off, Red," J. J. snaps back.

"Anyways," I say, "Our making a statement tonight will help ensure their support when it's really gonna be needed. Most of these students have only heard of the schools that we're gonna play. They don't understand that some of the schools we'll face in the Tri-County tournament are baseball recruitment centers for cheaters. So, the bigger the fan base we're able to take with us to the tournament field, the more viable energy we'll be able to use in every out we make, every run we score, and every win we earn—not just for Beaver Falls baseball, but for our community and the pride of Beaver Falls High School."

The bell rings, and this unusual lunch is over. But our mission for the Tri-County trophy just got a whole lot more interesting.

I tell everyone I'd either see them in the locker room or out at the field. I was off to my least favorite class, Spanish 4. The only thing I look forward to about this class is that the room it's taught in is over in the left wing of the high school. A shortcut there leads me past Mrs. Cooper's class.

Unless it's a test day, I always at least open the door for a quick "Hi" as I pass by Mom's classroom. Then there are moments when I lose track of the time allowed between periods because I was talking to Mom's fifth graders.

Usually Senora Diaz pays little attention to my tardiness. She knows Mrs. Cooper and the reasons I'm sometimes late. Besides, I am the only male student athlete in all of Spanish 4, which tends to help.

Today as I peek my head in to say hi to Mom my mother says, "Ricky, come in for a moment, there's something the kids would like to share with you."

"What is it?" I ask as I enter the room.

"Well, for last week's art project, the kids decided to make a banner to hang up for this evening's scrimmage," she says as she gestures toward the back wall of the room. A neatly constructed cardboard banner took up half of the back wall. Only Mrs. Cooper could have put something like this together using a bunch of short-attention-span fifth graders.

"Wow, how awesome!" Walking closer to the project, I point out a couple of things that make it stand out: I thank the class for thinking about Beaver Falls baseball. "The team will appreciate the pride and support of the Elementary Beavers." As I turn back, I see all the students twisted around in their chairs, most of them staring at me starry-eyed and blank faced. I decide to show my emotion and begin clapping in appreciation. Billy, our team bat boy, jumps up out of his seat a moment later and begins to do the same. The rest of the class follows suit. Knowing I have to get to Spanish class, I make my way to the door, but not without high-fiving every raised hand.

I jog from there into the left wing of the high school. I just make it in time before the tardy bell tones. I plant the ol' catcher's rear end into the seat of the desk and do my best to maintain focus on Senora Diaz.

I yawn a handful of times during Spanish. This is the only class where I have to force my wandering mind to stop thinking of baseball and instead respect the time Senora Diaz spends teaching. I listen to her instructions on the handwritten learning task reflected from the projector onto the screen. Forty-five minutes of continuous note taking can be a bit boring, but it also burns up the time. Soon the bell is sounding to send us out of sixth period and into my last subject of the day.

"Good luck tonight, Ricky," says Senora Diaz.

"Gracias," I say as I walk by her desk and out the door.

During the short walk down the hall to calculus, I hear someone yell "Beat Fox Lake Snatchers!"

Then I hear, "Put a dam in Fox Lake Crappers!"

I think to myself, "That doesn't make much sense." But knowing the voice of the source, I can only smirk and say, "Right on!" to Beaver Falls' oldest student.

Walking in the open-door classroom, I am surprised to see a young substitute sitting behind Mr. Varable's desk. "Hello," says the substitute, as I pretend not to notice her youth and good looks.

"Hello, ma'am," I keep walking to my seat, the other students filing in behind me.

"Ricky," says the sub.

I stop. "Yes, ma'am?"

"Ricky Cooper, right?" she asks. "I'm Mrs. Parker," she says as she stretches out her arm to shake my hand.

I'm still not sure what this was all about. I gently shake her slender hand as I say, "It's nice to meet you."

"It's an honor to formally meet you. My husband and son will be tickled that I had you in class today."

Not knowing how to respond to the remark, I ask, "Are they baseball fans?"

She laughs a little. "Oh, most certainly."

"Well, tell them I said hi and that I hope to see them at a game some time."

"Well, my son and I have plans to be at the game this evening."

"Super, what's your boy's name?" I ask the extremely attractive sub.

"Louie Jr." she said back. Then it hit me.

"You're the Backstop's wife?" I ask in anticipation.

"Yes, Ricky, I'm Mrs. Louie Parker."

I stand there for a second, speechless. I almost stutter as I say, "Ma'am, no disrespect, but what are you doing here filling in for Mr. Varable's calculus class for seniors at Beaver Falls High?"

"Well, I'm glad you asked," she says. "Louie and I bought a small farm just north of town to help keep him busy when he retires after this season's end. We both thought it would be best for Louie Jr. to be raised and taught here in Beaver Falls and to play baseball for his dad's alma mater."

"The Backstop is retiring?" I ask the question she has already answered.

"Yes. He's played the catcher position his whole amateur and pro career and, Ricky, you know what it does to a player's body." I nod my acknowledgment and she continues. "His goals after this season are to come back to Crossroad County, coach and mentor young Louie, and till the ground of crops on our farm. He wants Jr. and me to be here now so the boy can watch and learn from the best amateur catching prospect in the Tri-County and the team that surrounds him in their quest for the Tri-County trophy."

Standing there, trying to hold back the excitement that's causing every hair on my arms to rise, I say, "Mrs. Parker, thank you for sharing your husband's confidence in me and our team. I'll carry it with me throughout the season."

"You're quite welcome," she replies.

Walking away and to my desk, I'm not sure if the conversation was a confidence builder or pressure maker. But I thrive on both. I take my seat next to the smartest girl in class as I reflect on what I just learned. The Backstop's the guy I've tried to mimic my play on ever since I saw him outside the barbershop atop Mr. Ferguson's parade hay wagon, wearing shin guards and hoisting the Tri-County trophy. Now, the soon-to-be Tri-County Hall of Famer wants his son to watch and copy my play.

"Miss Calculus?" I say to the brainy girl sitting next to me.

"Yes, Ricky?" she replies.

"Please do me a favor and pinch me out of this dream of mine."

Miss Calculus proceeds to pinch me till I cry for mercy.

"Ouch! Ok, you can stop now," I tell the brainiac as she giggles.

"So where is Mr. Varable?" she asks.

"I don't know."

"Well," she says, "I thought during the conversation between you and the pretty sub, the subject of Mr. Varable's whereabouts would have presented itself."

"No, Miss Calculus. That lady there is the Goddess to the God of baseball itself and I just found out that she and her son are here to watch me play ball."

"And try to teach you calculus?"

"Well, we'll have to wait and see."

"Then maybe she can just try to help you comprehend the matter in the library next period."

I'm flipping through my textbook. "Why, Miss Calculus, is there a reason why you're not going to teach me your knowledge of the matter today?" But before she could answer, the substitute is asking for everyone's attention.

"Hi, class."

"She sure is high class," utters Miss Calc.

"My name is Mrs. Parker. Some of you probably know my husband, Mr. Louie Parker." Most of the class acknowledges their respect for the icon. She continues: "I'd like to apologize for my lack of expertise on the subject of calculus, so today all I'm going to have you do is pair up and review pages 93 through 97. Are there any questions?"

■ ■ ■

Even the best, at times, start to lose focus on what's in front of them. But the best just keep getting better the more they refocus and keep themselves from distractions life can put in a person's path—in this case, my calculus partner.

"Ricky, pay attention," says Miss Calculus.

"Ok. Sorry. You're right."

"So what's the next step here?" she asks as she's pointing her pencil at the long, drawn-out formula.

"Say, smarty...think we could talk a little baseball? We've been studying these problems for all of Calc class and half of this period here in the library."

"Absolutely," she replies and quickly flips closed the textbook.

"Wow," I say, "I should have asked you sooner."

"So, what about baseball?" she asks with a hint of excitement.

"I'll have to be honest with you, brainy; I didn't know you had any interest in baseball."

"Well, Ricky, I know only what my grandfather shared with me about the game."

"Oh yeah, what's that?"

"That you're the best all-around player he's ever witnessed at the high school level."

"Sure is a nice compliment from your grandfather."

"Yes, but he also says if you do have a weakness in your game, it's your speed around the bases." Before I can react to the slight knock, she says, "But grandpa says you make up for the flaw by being extremely consistent in your decision making while running the inside corners of the bags."

"For someone to know that, he must have played the game," I say.

"Yes, he did—and from what I've been told, he was quite the center fielder."

"Oh yeah, who is this grandfather of yours?" I ask with curiosity.

"His name is Walter Rawlings."

I was floored. "Hot damn! You mean to tell me that your grandpa is Stretch Rawlings?"

"Yes, you know him?" she asks.

"Know him?" I started to say, "Anyone associated with Beaver Falls baseball knows him."

"Really?" she asks.

"Yes, really."

"What can you tell me about him?"

"Well, first of all, I want to give you my sympathy for his passing away a few months back."

"Yeah, he didn't last long after Grandma's funeral. I guess love has a way of showing itself," she says as she looks down in grief.

"Well, that's why they put 'Together Again' under a recent photo of your grandparents on the obituary page of the Beaver Times," I say, trying to make some light of the subject.

"Yes, I guess so," she says as she looks up at me.

After a moment I ask, "Hey, you know why they called him Stretch?"

"No. Why?"

"Because he could stretch a single into a double."

"Meaning he was fast?"

"From what I've been told, he could fly."

"Does he hold any records?" she asks.

"His playing days were before any individual records were kept. The most important record was the team's wins and losses at the end of the season, but I'm sure if they had kept records, he would have been right around the top for steals and extra base hits. He never told you any of this, Miss Calculus?"

"No, he never talked about himself, just about current games and the players who stand out."

"How come you never came to a game with him?" I ask.

"I would always stay at home with Grandma and watch over her until he came back. She had lymphoma. But each time he came home from a game, he would sit and chat with us about it."

"That explains why he never stuck around after the last out. I almost thought he wanted to show how fast he could still get to his car." She smiles, and I ask if she wants me to continue.

"Absolutely," she says. "Please tell me more of what's been passed down to you from previous Beaver ball players and my grandfather's playing days."

4

"Hey, Red, do you have an extra cup?" asks Gunner.

"What the hell you asking me?" asks Red.

"You know. Something to protect our future Gunners," says Gunner as he grabs his crotch.

"No, but even if I did, my turtle snapper shell and strap would be way too big for your toy gunner."

"No, I just need the plastic piece. Not the wiiide strap that it goes in," Gunner grins as he makes a big, circular motion around his waist.

"Aww, real funny, asshole," says Red.

"Here," I say to Gunner as I toss him my extra dome cup.

"Great. Thanks, Fridge. Can't be too careful with the family maker," he says as he slides the protector into the jock strap he's already wearing.

With about three quarters of our team changing in the locker room, and everyone seeing what was happening, J. J. speaks up: "How can you guys share cups like that?"

"The same way your mom shares her cups full of double Ds!" says Red.

"Real funny, lard ass," J. J. shoots back.

As I finish lacing up my right cleat, little Billy walks in the male bonding room. "Mr. Cooper?" he says, "Granddad…I mean, 'Coach'…wants you in his office."

"Sure thing, Billy. I'm just finishing up here," I say as I'm straightening my uniform in front of the mirrored wall. As he walks out of the R-rated environment, I say "Hey, Billy?"

Stopping immediately, Billy says, "Yes, Mr. Cooper?"

"The banner that you helped make in Mrs. Cooper's class…"

"Yes?"

"Who wrote on the top left-hand corner, 'GO UNDEFEATED THIS SEASON!'?"

Pointing over to the half-dressed J. J., he says, "His sister."

"Ok, thanks, and again: good job on the banner," I say, giving him a thumbs-up.

I think for a moment while I'm standing there making sure I'm looking my best. I'm sure I'm going to use J. J.'s little sister's quote for part of my pregame speech. Right as Billy leaves and pulls the locker room door shut, it is pushed open by the live stockers themselves: the Oliver twins. Seeing Lefty waltz into the room followed by his brother, Righty, is reassurance of the possibility of going undefeated this season.

"Good to see you guys,"

"You didn't think we'd miss a game, even though it's only a scrimmage, did ya, Fridge?" asks Lefty.

"Well, your family's farm is the most important source of income you have."

"Yes, Fridge—until this here," he gestures with his left arm, "can provide the Olivers a little more laid-back style of living."

"It will, Lefty," I say. I grab my bat bag in one hand and the knuckles of the southpaw's right hand in the other. I turn to face Red. "Big, why are you three so quiet over there?

"Nothing, Fridge," One of the three says.

"Well, whatever you three amigos are up to, just don't make it obvious to the recipients."

"Come on, Fridge, we're better than that," says one of the stooges in the three-delinquent huddle.

"That's what I'm afraid of," I said to myself. Who knows what they're thinking up for our rival team.

Heading to the locker room door, I see that Jonas has made his way into the room. "Hey, Jonas." I walk over to where he is sitting down and taking off his generic Velcro tennis shoes.

"Oh, hey, Fridge," he says, but he isn't making any eye contact.

I recognize his body language. I pop a squat on the bench next to him. "Jonas, are you still not quite sure you're doing the right thing by being here?"

"Yeah, Fridge, sorry. I just cannot ignore my conscience."

"Well, save them 'sorries' for Mrs. Kuber. Do yourself a favor and do what's natural to you."

He glances down at the old, beat-up shoes he's worn while fielding thousands of ground balls and the new pair of team spikes sitting next to them. Then he looks back up at me. "What do you think the guys will say when I walk out there in my farm tennies?"

"Well, Jonas, they will laugh at first, until you show them it's not the shoes making the plays you are capable of—it's your raw talent."

"So you think I should wear them?" he asks.

"Just trust your instincts." I pat him on the thigh and get up to go see Coach. I am hoping Jonas will wear his trusty, crusty shoes. I would have told him sooner about the shoes, but it kept his mind from wandering elsewhere, like the crowd he is about to face for the first time while playing a game he was born to play. As I open the locker room door, I see Jonas opening his locker to find the copy of Red's picture that I pasted on the inside of the door. It shows Big sitting atop Elroy, bare chested, wearing his tighty-whities and barn boots, with reins in hand as if he is riding off into a pasture of pleasure.

I knock on Coach's door and hear the deep voice from within breathe the words, "You may enter." I slide open the door to Coach Gibbs's office and step inside. I don't think anyone else could be comfortable in the damp chill of the office but Coach. "Hey, Coach. Billy said you wanted to see me?"

"Yes, Ricky," he says, looking over his spectacles and motioning toward the lone empty seat.

"Thanks, Coach," I say, accepting the judgment chair and wondering why he sent for me.

"So, Ricky," he says, still sitting at attention and removing his glasses, "I suppose you don't know why I sent for you."

"Clueless," I say. "To help make out the lineup?"

"Well, Ricky, there's a couple of things I want to share with you—and of course, ask for your help with the lineup. This year is my last as head coach for Beaver ball. You see, Ricky, there comes a time in a man's life when he has to except the hand he's been dealt. Like this, for instance," he says as he raises his three-fingered pitching hand. "At one time, I had a lot of the same ability as you do for the game, except mine was as the opposite of the catcher. I had just as many scouts watching my games as you do now, and believe it or not, some were there to watch me pitch from the pro level.

"But I was drafted for another cause that claimed part of my hand. After returning home from the war, I tried to keep playing the game I loved. For a couple years, I held on because of a three-fingered knuckle ball that looked like a drunken butterfly with a pace of sixty-five miles per hour. But then I started losing feeling in the rest of the hand, and my butterfly soon cocooned back into a caterpillar."

"So that's what led me back here to my hometown to become head coach of the program that gave me opportunities through the game. It took me a few years to accept my role, but when I did, I started having just as much fun as I did when I used to stare down the catcher's mitt. As we started winning league titles and playing in the Tri-County tournament, I poured my love for the game into the young hearts that have helped make Beaver ball today. I would have liked to have won more Tri-County trophies, but ever since private schools were allowed to enter the tournament, it's been tough."

"My years here were numbered until you came along as a freshman. The opportunity to witness firsthand what you have brought to the field reignited my diminishing desire for the game. Martha and I already had plans for my retirement on the homestead, but I wasn't happy with the way I would have to part from the game I respect. So I decided to stick it out for your remaining years of eligibility."

"Last year, we were close to the goal we both have in common. With everyone coming back this year, including Bo, I thought the trophy would be all ours this year. But then we lost Bo to our worst rivals, Easton Prep, who are again the overall favorites to repeat as Tri-County champs. I was ready to give up again until you showed up at my residence ready to fight on. Ricky, you proved to me that day, even at my age, what we soon forget: we're never going to figure life out. The sooner we regain our focus, the sooner we can march on, despite life's unexpected casualties. Thank you, Ricky, for reeling me back in that day. I was about to throw in the towel."

I did not know the effect I had on Coach that day. "You're welcome, Coach. I've been fortunate to have the parents I do and their counsel."

"Yes. You know, Ricky...when your father was a student athlete here, his humor kept the morale of the team up, even when we had trouble finding enough players with real talent. I wish we had more to go with him then. Now that he's a successful business owner, he not only gives the best flattop in town—he also gives a bit of daily advice with a touch of sarcasm. Also, if you need to know the latest score of a game, he's your man. It's great to have him here in Beaver Falls.

"As for your mother, I can still see her sitting atop the bleachers, multitasking: watching the game your father was playing with a textbook centered on her lap. Anybody who could recognize love could see her and your dad's future together. Beaver Falls Elementary is most blessed to have her knowledge in the classroom teaching our young minds."

"Yes, she's one of a kind," I say.

"She sure is."

After a brief moment of silence, Coach says, "Now about that line-up."

■ ■ ■

After leaving Coach's headquarters, I walk down to the field. My attention is grabbed by Bucky, who is shagging some fly balls with the rest of the outfielders.

"Ricky," he says, running to the foul line where I'm standing.

"Yes, Bucky?"

"Can you make sure Coach has me batting in the ninth hole today?"

"Bucky," I say, "you are getting DH'ed today."

"DH'ed?" His expression couldn't be more stricken if he was kicked off the squad. "What for?" he asks.

"The same reason you want to bat last. Your confidence level is sour," I tell him.

"How am I supposed to build confidence if I don't get to swing the bat?" He asks.

"That's something you're gonna have to figure out for yourself."

"Ok, Fridge…good enough answer for me, but am I still starting right field?"

"For now," I tell him as I walk away.

I feel a little guilty about the short conversation with a fellow senior, a guy I grew up playing with. However, I have confidence in my strategy with the unsure Bucky. As I walk the baseline of the infield, I see Big Red is up to his ol' self. He's wearing a coonskin cap while fielding some ground balls.

"What took you so long?" Red asks as he sees me approaching.

"I'll explain to you later, Big, but for now, take that ridiculous hat off."

"Absolutely not," he replies while adjusting it back into place.

Reaching the dugout, I set my bat bag down, slide the zipper open, and grab my ritual bag of sunflower seeds. Popping a handful into the inside of my cheek, I am getting into my favorite mode: game mode. I take a deep breath and exhale a baseball player's prayer, I grab my mitt and join the fielding practice.

"Hey, Jr." I say to our first base coach who was hitting infield practice.

"Ah, hey, Fridge," he says while swatting another grounder.

"I got this, Herbie," I say as I motion for the ball from the shagger.

"All right, Fridge," he says and flips me the stitched rawhide.

Herb turns to join the rest of the infielders. "There's one more thing," I say.

He looks back. "Yeah, Fridge?"

"You're batting for Bucky in the ninth hole."

"All right," he says with excitement. He pumps his fist into his glove and trots off.

"You just made his day," Jr. tells me.

"I know he's just a sophomore, but he's ready to crack the line-up," I reply while Jr. smacks another ground ball.

After a few more grounders, Jr. says, "All right, let's throw it 'round."

Throwing the ball around is one of my favorite warm ups. The objective is for each player to take his position. Once you catch the ball, you must quickly and accurately throw it to the furthest position away from you, but not to the last one you received it from. If done right, this exercise is a great way to train players in maintaining their focus.

Usually, we get a few rounds in before Red forgets where to throw the ball, sometimes after a fan in short shorts walks in and catches his attention. Seeing Red move with a coon tail bobbing up and down out of the back of his unofficial hat is making this warm up even tougher to complete. Thankfully, Coach Gibbs emerges from the locker room, and it doesn't take long for him to holler at Big Red to "take off that Davy Boone hat."

"Ah, man!" says Red, "Those fur traders we're about to play aren't even here yet." He grabs the hat by its tail, gives it a few swings, let's go, and watches it land next to the visitors' dugout.

As we continue with our rapid-fire throws, I am starting to notice the early fans filtering in, as well as a peculiar smell circulating in the air by the wind.

"All right, boys, we all here?" Coach Gibbs says. "Let's get some cuts in."

"Red!" I shout. He looks up, and I say, "Give me a hand with the L-shaped screen." I point over to where it sits behind the visitors' dugout. The odor is only getting stronger as I approach the destination. As I reach the back of the dugout, I know Red had a part in this foul odor and I was about to find out the cause. "Dude!" I say to my best friend, "I thought I told you not to go overboard with a prank that is obvious, let alone one that burns the hair out of your nostrils."

Laughing, Big says, "Fridge, this is my senior campaign, and I'm gonna set a new mark for Beaver Falls' class clown. I'll do my best not to get caught while pulling off my feats. Besides, Fridge, I got the idea from your old man."

"My dad?"

"Yes, I overheard him at the Irish Schnitzel a ways back talking about the ol' fox-urine-extract-in-the-visitors'-dugout trick while he was tossing some suds back with some of the locals."

"How long have you known about my father's practical jokes when he was a teenager?"

"Teenager?" Red asks and shakes his right index finger side to side. "Mr. Cooper is still a funny Coop. Maybe you should learn some lessons about how to be a free spirit."

"Well, maybe you should show your dad a little more maturity, and he might start his conversations with you instead of me."

We stare at each other for a moment. Our silence is broken by our bond as best buds. Not even a true knock on each other's personalities is gonna keep us from laughing and high-fiving. "You almost had me there," we say at the same time. We pick up the screen and walk by the entrance of the dugout, laughing even more about what those fur spreaders were gonna have to endure during the game.

"Hold on, Fridge," says Red as he bends down, picks up his hat by the tail, and slides it into his back pocket. "Can you believe Coach called it a Davy Boone hat? It's a Daniel Crockett. Duh!" Red does not have a mind for history.

As we set down the L-shaped screen just about ten feet or so in front of the pitcher's mound, Coach Gibbs shouts, "Hurry it up, boys. We have about forty-five minutes before we have to share the field. The lineup is posted on the inside of our dugout, and I want you guys to be batting in the order in which you're listed. Motor, you're leading off."

"Hell, yeah, Coach! These legs are greased and ready to round some bases. Good choice, having me in the one hole."

"You can thank Ricky," says the coach. "It's his idea. Now grab a helmet and lay some bunts down." Walking away from the motor mouth, Coach then yells for Billy.

A handful of guys are surrounding the list posted on the wall. Most of them have an idea where they are going to fall in the line-up, but you still hear some say "Damn," and, "Why the hell am I batting there?" This happens before most games at any level if you have a team full of competitors, so I'm happy to hear a little bickering among my teammates.

"Red," I say, as he is still standing near me, "you're batting cleanup."

A look of surprise comes across his square jaw, until he manages to say, "About damn time!" as he looks in Coach Gibbs's direction with his hands clenched.

"Big, relax on the adrenaline a bit. You're there because of your off-season workouts and the commitment you've put toward our team."

"I could eat a fox cat right now, I'm so jacked!" he exclaims.

"Good," I say, "but save it for the plate of fastballs these fox furs are gonna try and blow by ya."

"You know it, Cooper," he says while adjusting his snapper shell.

"By the way, Fridge, where you gonna be?"

"I'm gonna be on base looking to score," I say with determination.

As I walk toward the dugout, I see Coach Gibbs has Lefty pulled to the side to tell him the game plan we have in store for the Trappers. I was hoping to see Lefty walk away from Coach looking positive about our strategy, but their conversation is going longer than I'd thought it would. I reach the dugout and pull "the Hammer" out of my bat bag.

I've used the nickname "Hammer" for my baseball bats for quite some time. Dad was working on a project at the house one summer just after my tenth birthday. When he came back out from a lunch break, he saw that I had taken the initiative to help pound some nails into the deck he was building for Mom.

"Son," he said, "What the hell are you doing?"

"Hammering nails, Dad," I said.

"With a ball bat?"

"Yeah, Dad. Watch this." Before he could stop me, I applied two whacks squarely to the head of that nail, pounding it flush against the board.

"Damn, Son," he said with a certain amount of surprise, "nice job, but don't ever frickin' do it again. That bat is for baseballs only."

It's still one of his favorite stories to tell in the barbershop today. Ever since then, the few bats that I've owned have always been referred to as "the Hammer." Anytime Dad wanted us to go hit some baseballs, he would tell me to go grab my Hammer.

Strapping my batting gloves on around my wrist, I walk out to the on deck circle just as Motor is taking his last cuts from Coach J.

"Hey, J. J." I say to the next man up.

"What's up, Fridge?"

"How's your arm?"

He grabs his right elbow. "My arm?" he asks as though he didn't hear me.

"Yeah, the thing that's connected to your right shoulder," I say as I point toward his right side.

"Feels good, Fridge. Why?"

"Because you're starting on the mound."

"What?"

"That's right," I say. "You're starting for us."

It is good to see the look of shock come across his face. "Why not Lefty?" he asks.

"Because the last time we played these guys, they knocked Lefty around pretty good and ended up beating us in the last game of the regular season. So today, you're our man. Ok?"

"Yeah. Sure thing, Fridge."

"Good, be ready for me to warm you up after I get done hitting. Ok, Junker?" I say as I slap his butt to send him toward the plate.

As I stand there stretching with my Hammer, I am mentally rehearsing the game plan that Coach and I put together. First, I want this game to be exciting for the fans who are walking in now and the rest who will come later. The home-field advantage is an opportunity that a lot of teams lose because they take it for granted. It starts before the game when the excitement is gathering as the fans come in. We should recognize them as part of our team's makeup. The more we accept the fans as part of the team, the better shot we have of hoisting the grand prize. Acknowledging some of the fans as they pass by on their way to the stands while I continue to stretch is part of my responsibility for ensuring they'll play their part.

Second, it will get everyone's hearts pounding for more if the game is close, at least for a while. That's one of the reasons I chose J. J. Junker as our starting pitcher. J. J. is the third man in our three-man starting rotation. He has decent stuff, and I can help by framing the strike zone. When he misses, it's chest high and meaty. His pitching will give us opportunities to get some practice in fielding and throwing the ball around a bit. Besides, we still have Lefty and Righty in our arsenal to replace him on the mound.

Also, bumping me up to third instead of in the cleanup role is hopefully gonna boost Big Red's focus at the plate because of the respect a player receives from opposing pitchers in the four hole—and chicks also dig cleanup hitters. Let's just hope this all goes as we planned it.

Speaking of the ladies' man, here he comes, jogging off the field, high and mighty, following his place in the lineup. After waving a couple more times at the people rolling in and swinging the Hammer a little, Red walks toward me and the on-deck circle with his chest pushing the buttons on his jersey to the max and almost popping them off.

"Man, Fridge, I'm feeling it," he says as he approaches me.

"Good," I say. "Just don't gain a hat size on me."

"No, Fridge, I won't, but I think I'm gonna need a bigger turtle shell," he says as he grabs his crotch for adjustment yet again.

"Sorry, Red," I reply, "but I gave my only backup to Gunner in the locker room earlier." Both laughing, we fist bump.

We're still laughing as he asks, "Did you hear Coach ask Coach Jr. if the porta potty pickup exchanged last year's silos of human waste for fresh ones this season?"

"No, but I know you had to counter with something to the comment you overheard."

"Yes, I did, Fridge. I told him the truth of the matter."

"And what was that?" I ask.

"When I finished up nabbing one of J. J.'s ground balls, I went over to the pair of coaches as they talked and told them the reason for the foul stench."

"You told them you put store-bought fox piss in the visitors' dugout?"

"Hell no!" he says, "I told them a stinky, wet fox cat decided to make its home in that there dugout, as I pointed to the visitors' hangout."

"You told them a 'fox cat' made that awful stank?"

"Yeah, Fridge, you know…that Siamese fox that's been wandering around here lately?"

"Unbelievable!"

"What do you mean by that?" he asks.

"It's unbelievable that you have yourself convinced that the smell coming from the stuff you personally put in the dugout is actually coming from a Siamese fox cat."

"Ya," he replies as though he's surprised I didn't know this.

"Anyways, Fridge, what's our game plan for these fur pissers?"

As I stand there, only telling him what he needs to hear, his concentration is soon distracted by a few of Beaver Falls' finest grinning in our direction as they walk by. "Have you ever seen so many so early?" he says as he looks at his favorite temptations and then over toward the rest of the fan base already here.

"Never." I snap my fingers to regain his limited focus. "Red, this is one of our most important games of the season." I try to impress on him why this game means so much for everyone here, not only for those of us on this side of the fence playing the game.

J. J. is finished with his twenty-pitch maximum, and it is my turn to step up into the right side of the chalked lines of the batter's box. . Hitting is an art that talented players can learn through knowledgeable instruction and repetition. I have an advantage, a natural ability to see the actual contact of wood on leather at a high speed.

"Let's see some long balls, Fridge," I hear the voice of an older fan say, probably sitting about three rows deep. Any hitter with decent power can show off a bit during batting practice. This is why some of the fanatics show up early to a scheduled ball game: to see long ball hitters connect with short-distance pitches tossed by a soft arm.

Coach Jr. knows where my "wheelhouse" is, so I don't have to say a word to him. I simply give him a nod and gesture with the Hammer to ask for some grooved pitches. I watch his arm. His release point is spot-on for a ball that wants a new owner. After I bomb a few and notice some scouts taking notes while talking among themselves, I ask Coach Jr. to throw me some hangers.

Hitting a good curve is one thing, but stroking a great curve to right field will get these next-level scouts to stop the chitchat, put their pencils and pads down, and regain focus on the hitting display that's being put on in front of them. As Coach Jr. delivers his right-handed hanger, I can see the stitches on the baseball rotate. I rock my weight forward and then back to my right side, loading up the power generator. I feel electricity from the earth penetrating my right foot and rapidly climbing up my whole right side. I remain calm and focused, with my hands tucked back. I'm waiting to flip the switch. "Wait, wait," I tell myself. Then, as the ball is at its final breaking point, I unleash the electrified hammer with an inside-out swing and show what scouts at any level of play love to see: a right-handed hitter ignite a curve ball over the right-field wall.

Deciding that was my last swing before the game, I walk away from home plate with applause coming from the stands. I grab another fist bump from Red as I walk by the number-four man. "Look," I say as I point back to the applauding fans, "they're welcoming you to the plate." As big as his grin is, I almost believe he thinks I was serious. I make my way to the dugout and quickly begin slapping my catcher's gear on to go warm up J. J.

Meanwhile, Jonas, who is batting fifth, comes off the field and into the dugout. He sets his glove down and then sits next to me on the bench. "Sure are a lot of people out there, Fridge."

"Jonas, you'll be fine. Don't let them get into your head."

"Actually, they're not the ones really in my head."

"I'm not sure what you're telling me, Jonas."

"Well, there are these voices already in there that are trying to tell me that I don't belong here."

"When did these inside influences start trying to persuade you out of your given talent?" I ask him.

"Just recently," he says.

"Jonas, you've never heard these critics' voices before?"

"No, Fridge, honest—just recently."

Reaching over and grabbing Jonas by the arm with a firm grip, I look directly into the young man's eyes. Knowing I have his full attention, I tell him, "The next time you hear those devilish voices, you tell them Ricky Cooper says to go back to hell." Finally feeling a sense of relief stemming from Jonas, I soften my grip and let go of his arm.

After I snap my last shin guard in place, I grab my mitt and take off to the cages to warm up J. J.'s arm. As I turn the corner of the dugout, I see J. J., Lefty, and Righty leaning against the cage, laughing it up. This is a welcome sight, especially the competitive Lefty. As I approach them, I hear Righty telling the other two about how Red set the scene for his fox urine prank.

"Hey, Fridge, you're just in time to hear the explanation Red gave coach about the foul odor coming from the visitors' dugout," says Lefty.

"I already heard about the Siamese fox he laid the blame on."

"Yeah," Righty says, "but he really went out of his way with this one."

"There's more to it?" I ask.

"Sure is," says Righty. "Red took the initiative to have posters made up of this so-called dugout peeing perpetrator.

"Posters?"

"Ya, poster boards with all different sayings on them that he and Gunner strategically placed coming up the street to the school."

"I've never known Red to be strategic about anything," I say.

"Well, I did overhear him tell Coach—who was rolling his eyes and walking away—not to worry, because he had the smell covered."

"Yeah, I figured Coach knew the difference between actual fox odor and the fake fox urine hunters use that you can buy down at Gunner's dad's store."

"There's still more, Fridge," says Righty.

"What now?" I ask.

"Well, he and Gunner skipped their last two classes of the day and rounded up some not-so-willing country fox to let loose sometime during the game."

"Man," I say, "he really does have a plan."

"Yes, he does," says a laughing J. J.

"So, where is this caged lion cat?" I ask.

"Red wouldn't share that one. He's leaving it as a surprise."

"Let's just hope he remembers he still has a baseball game to play," I say. "Now, let me tell you guys the plan I've drawn up for our competition." I explain the plans and feel as though we are all on the same page. The four of us stand in a huddle. We raise our fists to the center and touch them together, saying simultaneously, "Beaver ball!" That is all the reassurance I need.

■ ■ ■

"Damn, J. J.," I say after catching his fastball, "that ball has got some great movement today." I want to build his confidence. "Throw a couple more of them, and then start throwing some benders."

"Sure thing, Fridge," he says as he adjusts his ball cap. A couple of scouts approach the outside of the cage.

"Hi, Ricky," says an overweight ex-ballplayer.

"Oh, hey there, Brownie," I say.

"So, Ricky…you ready for another season?" he asks.

"Yes sir," I say as I continue to warm up J. J.

"Ricky," says Brownie, "I know I've been after you to sign a letter of intent to come play for us since the beginning of last year, and I do apologize for the constant bothering, but I have here someone I'd like to introduce you to." Standing next to Brownie is a gentleman in much better shape than his counterpart, but I can tell he was around the same age. "Ricky, this here is Pete Gambler, better known as RBI Pete."

I almost miss a decent curve ball from J. J., but managed to snow cone it while coming out of the catcher's squat to get a better view of the famous player. "Hello, sir," I say, looking at the bright-eyed, retired third baseman. Removing my catcher's mask and lid, I ask, "Mr. RBI Pete, to what do we owe the honor of your being here?"

"Ricky Cooper," he says, "you're as well versed as advertised. Thank you for the acknowledgment. Let me have the honor of finally being introduced to you and your wall of accomplishments," says Mr. RBI.

"Thank you, sir, and welcome to Beaver Falls Baseball."

Brownie says, "Pete and I played together a few years back and a couple pounds ago," he says as he rubs his round waist.

I am a little surprised. "Is that right?"

"Yes, we did," says Pete.

"Of course, Pete went on to play in the majors," says Brownie, "and I bounced around a little until I found my talent for scouting fine young men such as yourself. Anyways, Ricky, we see you're busy warming up your starter, so maybe after the game Pete and I could talk to you a little more about coming and playing for us."

"Yeah, sure thing," I say, addressing both of them.

"One more question, Ricky," asks the rotund scout.

"Yes?"

"Why aren't you guys starting Lefty Oliver?"

"Because we need the fielding practice," I say.

"Ok, then, and good luck today, Ricky."

"Thank you, Brownie," I say as I slide my mask back on over my lid, squat back down, and give J. J. a target.

After a few more pitches, J. J. asks, "Who was the guy with Brownie?"

"Pete Gambler," I tell him.

"Holy fox urine!" says J. J. "That was RBI Pete?"

"Yep, the one and only," I say.

"What's he doing here with Brownie?" he asks.

"Bait," I say.

"Bait?"

"Yes, a recruiting method."

"Wow," says J. J., "Brownie bringing the RBI king here is a hell of a recruitment lure."

"Yes, it sure is," I reply while trying to hide a smile.

Squatting there and finishing up with J. J., I can't help but think how far that very respectable program is willing to go to get me to come play the game I love for them. I mean, I know Brownie has been after Lefty, me, and last year's shortstop, Bo, for quite some time. Our guys have gotten used to seeing him at games. But for them to send their elite as a recruitment tool is a high honor. I'm extremely proud for Lefty and me.

As I catch J. J.'s last warm up, I say to him, "If you pitch like this during the game, some of these scouts may be keeping an eye or two on your right arm."

"You mean it, Fridge?" he asks.

"Yeah, J. J. Would I bullshit you about a tailing fastball you somehow developed?"

"What's my fastball doing?" he asks.

"Never mind," I say. "Just keep doing what you're doing during the game.

"Sure thing, Fridge," he says with another cap adjustment.

Walking out of the cage with J. J., I see that my dad and Greeny Mowit, our school's groundskeeper, are hanging Mom's fifth-grade banner on the inside of the left field home run fence. My dad and Greeny go back to their days as sandlot swingers. They grew up together as teammates and tag-team partners. Some say they were a naughty one-two punch. Or maybe it's just Greeny reminiscing about their glory days while sucking down twelve-ounce ambers in the barbershop during and after his once-a-week trim.

Dad never agrees or disagrees with the loudmouth. He just grins and keeps on snipping, taking a casual sip here and there from his own beer. As for the Trappers, their bus has just turned the corner and is moseying up the street. My adrenaline always starts to flow when I first see our competition, whether it's them rolling in on a bus, or us pulling up in one. J. J. interrupts my buzz with a bump from his elbow and says something about Red's signs lining the low-speed-limit street.

"Either way J. J., you just remember to handle the baseball the way you did in warm-ups. This team of fur backs can hit."

"Coach!" I shout. After I see I have his attention, I point to the arsenal of enemy hitters and say, "They're here."

"Round it up, boys!" yells Coach Gibbs, "It's time to share the diamond."

"Oh, hell yeah!" Red bellows out.

5

"Would you take a look at that fox?" says Red. Most of us have our backs turned, so we quickly wheel around, thinking we'll see the upset four-legged critter scampering across the field. But instead he was indicating a rare "ten" on the foxy/hot scale. "Gentlemen," he says, "that woman there would make the local priest take off his collar."

As she waits for her driver to step out of an expensive car you rarely see in these parts, she is brushing back her dark brown hair with her hand. The sundress she is wearing is a light peach sheet barely covering up perfection. Most of us are doing what baseball players do and rearranging our now-uncomfortable jocks and cups.

"Do you think she knows all of us are over here drooling over her beauty?" asks a quiet Finn.

"Absolutely, she does," says Red.

"Explain your analysis," says Bucky.

"That's easy," explains Red. "First, any time a lady gets out of a two-door sports car like that on her own, she wants everyone to know she's available. Women who are happy with their significant others wait for them to come around and help them out of the passenger car door. Second, I guarantee the bum she's with is some big shot loser who's talking into a flip phone that's plugged into the center console. Third, if she sits down against the front end of the shiny, new car with her arms folded with a look of desperate need for attention, she's as easy to pick up as your ground ball, Bucky. Finally, the icing on the cake is if she reaches into her pocket purse, pulls out a long, skinny smoke, and eases her frustration by lighting up."

"How the hell do you know all this?" asks Buzzy.

Red simply points to his eyes then out and says, "By maintaining focus on my surroundings, and by watching Mrs. Junker get out of a car."

Patting the big man on the back, I say how proud I am of him.

Jonas speaks up. "Sure beats what we call proper attire."

We all start laughing as the scene plays out just as Red predicted using his crystal ball, right down to the icing on the cake. After a moment, we all go back to playing pepper.

As they make their way off the bus, we can already hear a chorus of boos showering the Trappers. The jeers get louder as the rival team makes its way through the gates and down the right field line.

Most of our student fans are hanging out by their parked cars having a pregame party. I can tell Mustang is the ring leader out there. The oil back has the nicest horse in town, and he and Sally can really throw a party of any size. One thing about Sally is that her parents own Beaver Falls' Grocery, so since middle school, whenever she and Mustang would have any type of get together, they always had an abundance of food and other refreshments.

Our ball park is laid out with the parking lot behind center field. Our school sits off a bit behind left field. Behind right field is the visitors' parking lot and the porta potties. Behind the infield is the seating, and behind them is the Land of Lost Balls. This consists of a few trees but is mostly the marshland that the area's busy beavers have made for us. The town's named "Beaver Falls" for a reason.

I see the Trappers are about to catch a whiff of Big Red's "fox cat" as they approach their home for the next seven innings. Falling out of pepper ball, I tell the guys, "I'll be right back," because I have to visit right field and the portable toilets.

"Right now?" asks Red. "Them fur sniffers are about to get a nose full."

"Yeah, Red, but my bladder is acting like a dam holding back a flood of piss."

"All right," he says with a little disappointment, "I've got the same feeling of pressure backing up. I'll follow you over there."

As we're walking, Red and I keep looking over our shoulders. We finally see the Trappers stop dead in their tracks and look at one another with a grim acceptance of their plight as visitors. A couple of them are pointing back toward the street as if they're remembering the warnings on the signs they passed on the way in. "Those guys pointing and unsure of the play zone they're now in must be rookies," I say to Red.

"You've gotta love fresh fur," says Red. "Anyways, Fridge, why are we walking across the outfield to release the river?"

"You don't smell them hot dogs being grilled up in the center field parking lot by our student fans?"

"No, not really. I still have a little dribble of fox urine across my knuckles."

"Well," I said, "my hunger has strengthened my bladder control, and we're about to thank our supporters by stopping by for a couple of hot dogs."

A few minutes and a couple of dogs later, Big and I rejoin the guys to finish up pepper practice. This is a simple warm up we're just using to kill some time before the competitors get their chance for some fielding practice. All you need is a bat and ball and groups of five with their position gloves. You toss the ball at the hitter, who's using a choked-up grip, while the other four are a few feet apart and field the easy hits. This also works on your reflexes as you react to the ball coming off a soft-swinging stick.

Motor questions me and Red about eating hotdogs, especially just before a game.

"I'll let Red answer that for ya, Motor."

Red looks at him and says, "Because I can't get enough of lips and ass, whether it's between a couple of buns at a ballpark, or in a lunch line, or hell, even in the front of Ruby. I can eat them anytime, anywhere."

"We're still talking about hot dogs, aren't we?" asks Motor between the taps of the bat.

"Yes, ground-up scraps of meat rolled into a link," says a smiling Red.

"Look at them huddled up over there," says Gunner as he points at our adversaries.

"Yeah, knowing our rivals, they're probably plotting some type of revenge," I say.

"How do you think they'll retaliate?" asks Jonas.

"Not quite sure, but one of us is probably gonna get beamed."

"I hope it's me," says Buzzy. "Maybe that'll show my commitment to the team." Nobody pays much attention to his remark. We keep peppering.

With about half an hour before the singing of the anthem, fans from both sides are still steadily filing in, adding to my motivation to play great.

"Look," says Gunner, "they're using some type of aerosol spray in their dugout."

"Well, they better hope they brought the whole box with them to cover up the ol' Siamese fox's tracks," says Red.

"Those girls are probably using some type of lavender spray," says Gunner.

"Let's just hope it doesn't spark a chemical reaction with Red's fox scent," I said.

"Why not?" asks Gunner.

"Because I want to blow these guys up on the field, not in their dugout."

"Oh, hell yeah!" says a chest-beating Red.

Then everybody who had a pair—including my dad and Greeny, who were still hanging out by the banner—stopped and stared at

Miss Perfect as she paraded her sway of elegance up foul ball territory to the stands. "I'm in love and I don't even know her name," says Red softly.

It's a few moments before J. J. says, "I'm sure she doesn't know your name, either."

Red, still staring at the object of his desire, says, "Real good one there J. J. How long did it take you to think of that one?"

With a quick slap to Red's hindquarters, I tell him, "Remember what we're here for."

"All right, guys," I say, gathering everyone's attention, "let's break off into four-man relays." Four-man relays look easy from a spectator's view, but this drill relies on focus, command, athletic ability, and a good partner. We usually keep the same groups, but this time, Buzzy wants to get in with me, Red, and Jonas by switching teams with Fin. Buzzy and Fin both look at me for approval for the switch.

"Guys, I'm team captain and not your dictator, so if you guys want to switch it's your call," I tell them. Meanwhile, I am surprised that Buzzy wants to be in the middle with our four-man team. The guys decided to make the change.

Sometimes we make a race out of this warm up, but on game days, we're just looking for consistency and camaraderie. A four-man relay stands in a straight line, each about fifty feet apart, with one baseball per group. The ball starts at one of the bookends, which are Red and me in our group. The teammate with the ball throws it to the next teammate. He then catches it, turns, and fires to the next guy, who catches it and does the same. We do this back and forth as quickly and error-free as we can. Again, when done right, it's a great pregame routine to ready yourself to always be on your toes and to rely on your teammates' accuracy.

Red stands with his back to the decorated seats and begins the drill by throwing to Jonas. The ball is in my glove almost immediately. I quickly reach in and pull it out. By the time I have it cocked and ready to fire, I have the laces in the perfect place to deliver a throw to Buzzy's glove side.

I start to get the feeling that Buzzy might be back on board for some reason or another.

We aren't racing the other groups, but if we were, we'd be unbeatable. As the other groups drop balls, they stop to watch us display a four-man relay performed flawlessly. Back and forth we go, and each time we just keep throwing harder and harder. This is by far the longest and quickest relay I've ever been a part of, but it is soon ended when a "Siamese fox" painted in our school colors runs freely down the section of right center field the Trappers are occupying.

This might even top Red's squat record performance. Between the urine scent in the dugout, the signs placed along the street, and now an actual fox scampering past and throughout the Trappers, this definitely sets the record for Red's goal of being Beaver Falls High's best-ever class clown. Seeing the fox zig and then zag between its Trapper enemies is absolutely hysterical. The first thing was the trapper in pinstripes with the number twenty stitched on the back. This wussy preceded to take off running toward their school fur hauler screaming, "I think it tried to bite me." Another one squatted down just like grade school students are made to do during a school tornado drill.

Watching the Trappers holding their noses while trying to avoid the painted fox is the icing on Red's prank cake. He just stands there glowing with pride at his pregame accomplishment.

All but the Trapper's criminal pitcher were ducking in fear. Pottsy was making some nice moves on the estranged fox while looking like he was trying to wrestle it up.

"You should have brought some traps with your bats, you fur skinners!" yells Gunner.

This lasts for a good minute before the fox safely and successfully finds an escape route through a gate that my father had opened on the right side of the visitors' dugout. The colorful *fox cat* disappears into the marshland leaving behind no trace of foul play by Red McStein.

The Trapper's left fielder, the closest opposing player to our final warm up, looks over at us and asks, "How long have you had a problem with the school-colored stink sprayer?"

Gunner replied, "Ever since you northerners came south!"

We all laugh. With the field clear of the four-legged varmint and everyone settling down, it is about time for the captain's pregame speech. "Hey, Coach," I say to the stone-faced Gibb as he approaches the squad.

He stops. "Ricky, come here for a minute," he says

"Sure thing, Coach." Thinking he might be a tad upset about the fox folly, I jog over to where he's standing.

"Ricky," he says, "I don't want to put a feather in Red's hat and give him more motivation for his immaturity, so just between us, that was the greatest stunt ever pulled off, and when this season is over, I want you to tell Red I said so."

"Right on, Coach. Will do."

"Now, Ricky, this is your team, so I'm just gonna head back to our dugout and get the score book together."

As he turns to walk away, I say, "Hey, Coach…"

"Yes, Ricky?" he says, turning back.

"Thank you for sharing with me the ins and outs of why you're here today. I promise to you, at season's end you will be lifted up onto the shoulders of winners the way great coaches ought to be by grateful players."

"Ricky, that truly would be the cherry on top for my retirement." Before walking away, Coach gives me a rare fist bump as acknowledgement of a new trust between a young player and a veteran coach. Turning and looking at my responsibilities, I see a couple of our guys are playing grab butt, Gunner is still pointing and laughing at the Trappers, and Red is staring at another prize. I inhale a deep breath of confidence and exhale it toward my team.

"Team," I say, demanding attention, "let's take a knee." Sobering up quickly, everyone takes a knee. "Guys," I begin, "I want everyone to look down at the front of your jerseys." I wait for all their chins to drop and then I pause for a second. "Ok, now I want you to look at each other's jerseys. You see, this is why teams of any sort wear uniforms. It unites a team together as one. It signifies our commitment and allegiance to a program. This is our program: Beaver Falls baseball. Remembering the great players who have worn the same jersey, we need to take the highest pride in what we're here to do, and that's to play as a team and win.

My goal from when I was a little kid until today has been to win the Tri-County tournament. I want us to parade that silver award back down Main Street as victors. We will accomplish this feat by aiming our sights on a new target: going undefeated. At season's end, if we are 25 and 0, the silver trophy and the honor of the right to say we always had a winning score will be ours. The trophy has been won by Beaver baseball twice before, but no Beaver Falls High has put a 25 and 0 season in the record books."

"Yes, Bucky?" I say in response to the owner of the group's only raised hand.

"Ricky, you mean '24 and 0,' because we have an eighteen-game regular season schedule, and to win the tournament takes six games. That's a total of twenty-four, right?"

"Bucky, this scrimmage today won't be in the official school record books. So, yes, you're right." I say. "Mr. Thesaurus," I'm thinking to myself.

"What a dork," says Red.

"Guys, listen," I say. "To go undefeated will take more self-discipline and will mean we have to get better each and every day. Most of us have done well preparing ourselves during the off-season. The morning workouts, the evenings spent together down at Jonas's makeshift ball field, and our recent practices are all part of what winners do."

Seeing a few guys get antsy, I think, "I better wrap this up."

"So as team captain, I ask all of you to play together, maintain focus on your self-discipline, and to remember: an undefeated season is the ultimate prize. Now let's bring it in," I say as I stand up, "and 'Beaver ball' on three." With all our fists bunched together in the center of our huddle, I give the nod to Red. In a deepest voice and a tone that's almost frightening, he counts to three, and then we all shout, "BEAVER BALL!"

"Nice speech, 'Coach,'" says Red as we follow the team to the dugout.

"Wasn't too much, was it?" I ask.

"No. Other than Mr. Stats correcting you on the official number of games, I was impressed by your first pep talk as captain. You almost kept my mind from that brunette's beauty."

"I'll take your almost," I say. "Red, one more thing…"

"Yeah?"

"Why does it seem like Buzzy is now committed to being a team player?"

"Well, Fridge, that's because I had my own pregame pep talk with the hothead myself," he says with a slight grin.

I see my dad standing behind our dugout while other spectators are walking by to their seats.

"Hey, Mr. Coop," says Red. "Thanks for your help with the crazed fox sprinter."

"Sure thing, Red. It's one of those cases of being smarter than your average calico fox."

"Dad, you didn't happen to have a hand in the fox stunt, did you?"

"Well, Son, other than my hand on the visitors' side dugout gate, no, but there was a time I might have had more involvement in such a classic scene."

"So I've been hearing," I say softly while looking away toward the stands. Then I ask if Mom made it in yet.

"No, not yet, Son. She had a faculty meeting after class, but she told me to give you her best. She also gave me the banner to hang there in left center. Your mom, Ricky, sure adds a nice touch of class." says Dad as he admired the demonstration of his wife's ability neatly hanging on the home run fence.

"Say, Mr. Cooper," Red chimes in, a wad of gum rolling around in his mouth, "why don't you and your better half come in to The Irish Schnitzel this evening for dinner? The McSteins are throwing a little after-game celebration for the start of the season. Mrs. McStein...I mean, Mom...is giving a bottle of fine German Riesling to every set of players' parents who show up." Slapping me across the chest, Red says, "Maybe I can get ol' knock blocker here to stick around the Schnitzel's kitchen for some dishpan hands, and give ol' Mom and Dad a nightcap."

I'm shaking my head while my dad says, "Thanks, Red, for the gesture. It's been a bit since I've had some of that."

"Oh man, would you two cut it out," I say, still shaking my head.

"Son, I meant I haven't set my lips to some good German Riesling wine in a while. Your mom and I's love life is just as arousing as the early days, when we had to share each other on the only bed we could afford: a twin mattress with a broken spring."

This causes Red to light up with laughter, my head to continue shaking, and my dad to admire the banner in left center. With the school's color guard making their way down to the field I fist bump Dad as he demonstrates his usual advice by pointing to his eyes without saying a word. Returning a slap to Red's chest, I say, "Let's rock."

Team captains always stand next to home plate as the team lines up (down the third base line if you're at home, or down the first base line if you're the visitors). At our home field, the guest performers for the anthem stand near the captain. They are usually singers who were cast out of some garage band or another who still think they're better than the group. In this case, I am taken aback by the beautifully manicured, fashionably dressed Miss Calculus walking toward home plate with her head held high and the microphone in her hand.

As she makes her way to my favorite position behind the plate, so does a lot of people's attention. Standing there before the start of the anthem's background music, she notices my undivided attention, which by now she has learned to recognize, and gives me a slight wink. Accompanied by the music, she sings the words to our anthem with the utmost respect in a captivating soprano voice. The last lyrics seem to come too soon as she belts out the final note, stretching it out and leaving it hanging there along with everyone else's heartfelt imagination.

If the fans had brought flowers with them, they would have showered her with them in praise. As they are giving her a standing ovation instead, I begin to feel my heart race with uncertainty. Speechless, I can only look at the girl I thought I knew, and unfortunately can only give her a simple thumbs-up for the spectacular performance.

"Ricky," I hear, but don't really register.

"Fridge?"

Realizing the umpire is trying to retrieve my attention from my calculus tutor, I snap back with focus.

"Ricky," says the giant, gap-toothed man in umpire pants, "How many innings?"

"Seven," I say after my mind refocuses. "Seven is the number that Coach Gibbs and the opposition agreed on," I say.

"Seven?" he asks.

"Yes, seven," I say to the man who would love to get a full-time salary for this part-time job.

"This is a scrimmage right?" asks the disgruntled umpire, who was probably thinking this was gonna be a quick twenty-five bucks and an early bar stool.

"Yes sir, a scrimmage that we intend on winning," I say.

Mumbling, he walks away to meet with the field ump. Glancing at the visitors' stands, I am surprised by the limited number of empty seats left for a fanatic Trapper fan's backside. Fox Lake loves their Trapper baseball, but the town is about a forty-five minute commute to get here.

Turning my eyes to the seats full of Beaver ball fans, I see that Mom has made it to her usual place just down from the other moms, where she has the best view of home plate. Most of the moms sit together, so they can talk between innings about an array of topics outside baseball.

Numerous times I've overheard conversations while warming up the pitcher that I shouldn't repeat, but mostly they've been about their husbands' short endowments, small shoe sizes, and big beer bellies. Sitting just down from Mrs. McStein are Mrs. Parker and the Parkers' stocky offspring. My dad, along with a few others, likes to stand close to the dugout and talk about the good ol' days and how they didn't always have to suck in their guts for pictures.

Aware now of my surroundings, I jog into the dugout to grab my glove, helmet, and mask, and also to grab a peak at the lineup we're about to face. An adrenaline-filled dugout is an environment that I know I'll remember, even when I'm the one standing next to a dugout at a high school baseball game and talking about the good ol' days: I love it.

"They're throwing Potts at us," says J. J. Pottsy has always had a reputation as a loose cannon. Ever since the days of little league, he has been in and out of juvenile rehab for mischief.

I already know who their starter is because I saw the Trappers warm up earlier. "Ya, he must have finally got out of the juvenile detention home," I say.

"What criminal act landed him there this time?" asks an eavesdropping Lefty.

"Don't know but I'm sure it had something to do with a book of matches," says an equally eavesdropping Red.

"Last time we faced this delinquent, he got tossed for taking a swing at the umpire," says a passing Righty.

"What got him so fired up?" asks Jonas.

"Ball and strike calls," says Fin.

"No, guys, the reason he was put away for a while was because he beamed his cousin at a family reunion, which started a brawl that ended with him being hauled away in handcuffs," I say.

"They were probably fur cuffs," adds Red.

"What are fur cuffs?" asks Motor, who looks up while lacing his running shoe.

"I don't know," says Red, "Ask J. J."

"Why J. J.?" asks Bucky.

"Because his mom has a pair hanging from her rearview mirror." Everyone laughs except J. J.

I scan the Trappers' lineup in our scorebook. I remember most of the guys' weaknesses at the plate, as well as their wheelhouse. I ask Coach Jr. to scan last year's scorebook for stats from the last game we played against the Trappers. They're always a hard-hitting team, especially batters one through five.

Hanz Mueller is their lead-off man and also their starting center fielder. He and a couple of us have played some Tri-County all-star games together. He's guaranteed to play in the next level, and has a shot at the elite level. Mueller is a three-tool player, meaning he can run, hit, and throw his way around the diamond.

Other than having most of the same attributes on the field, we also have the same desire for forage. The Mueller's are patrons of the Irish Schnitzel from time to time. Once, Red and I saw Hanz wolf down about a dozen sausages with a speed that would make any resident of Frankfurt proud.

The Trappers also have a heavy-hitting cleanup man who plays third base. He has been shaving since the sixth grade. Everyone calls him "Razor."

Another guy to keep off balance is their starting shortstop, Shorty Glover. What he lacks in size, he makes up by swinging a big one. I've seen him hit some monster shots on mistake pitches.

Then you still have to pitch to Pottsy, who holds the record among high school players for charging the mound.

I hear the bellow from the umpire for the players to take the field. Normally, I'm 100 percent committed to what lies ahead, but today I have a rare feeling. A bit of my attention is not on the game; it's still on Miss Calculus.

6

I catch J. J.'s last warm up pitch and make a snap throw to Jonas, who is covering second base. I slide my mask up, turn to the game regulator, and say, "We're good."

He spits out a mouth full of minted manure and yells, "Play ball!" The words echo throughout the field. Whatever distractions that were present in anyone's mind are now replaced with the reasons why we're here.

Hanz walks up to the plate with his bat and a face full of determination.

"Mueller," I say in acknowledgement.

"Cooper," he returns the same.

I send some hand signals to the team. I silently point to left field and slowly move my finger all the way over to right field. Our guys should already know that Hanz Mueller is capable of taking the ball where it's pitched, but I make it a habit to alert our squad about the strengths of every batter who steps up to the plate.

When I see that all our players are positioned well, I slide my mask down and over about a week's growth of facial hair, get into my catcher squat, and call for an outside fastball by pointing to the inside of my right thigh with my middle finger. J. J. gives me a nod of acceptance and starts his windup. The pitch catches the outside corner for a strike, with Hanz swinging and missing. Inside my mitt, my palm feels like I just caught one of Lefty's pitches. I'm a little surprised by J. J.'s heat.

"All right! Nice pitch!" says someone in the crowd, and I hear some scattered applause.

The look I get from Hanz is priceless.

"When did J. J. develop a tailing fastball?" he asks.

"Just today," I say as I fire the laced rawhide back to the pitcher.

"Nice pitch," he says as he climbs back into the box and digs in. "I won't miss that heater on the outside corner again."

I already knew he wouldn't, either. I give a tap to the inside of my left thigh to call for the same pitch on the inside of the plate. J. J. agrees then rocks into his windup. He paints the inside corner, and the umpire calls, "Strike two!"

This really gets the crowd stirred up. Hanz kicks up some dirt in disgust. I grin as I throw the ball back to J. J.

As Hanz steps back in to the box with a confident swagger, I sense he is expecting another fastball—and that's exactly what we're gonna give him. Tapping the inside of my left thigh, I give J. J. the signal for the same pitch. I would usually call for an off-speed pitch here, but if J. J. starts this game out by throwing three fastballs past one of the Tri-County's better hitters, it would bring out a roar from our Beaver backers, and momentarily silence the Trapper chatter.

As the stitches roll off J. J.'s finger tips, I can hear Mr. Junker yell, "That's my boy," from a distance. Then the sound of the umpire ringing up Hanz Mueller on a perfect fastball that rubbed the inside corner sings in our ears.

Firing the out down to third base and watching the team throw it around the infield never felt better. Hanz never strikes out, let alone without swinging on the last pitch. It could be his first-ever backward K for the scorebook.

The Beaver fans are roaring with appreciation; the Trapper backers are as silent as a fox hunting its prey. As the crazed Beaver ball fans settle down from the punch out, J. J. is already standing on the rubber, waiting for his next victim: Shorty Glover. Shorty is a dead-pull ball hitter and loves the inside pitch. I again alert the left side of the field to his strengths and have the right side shift a little to their right. The field is set to defend. I call for Shorty's weakness by throwing down two fingers for a curve and then a palm down to the right side of the plate, meaning "Keep it low and away." J. J. takes the call and delivers the pitch down and a bit too far away, for his first ball call. Tapping the inside of my right leg, I ask for the same pitch. J. J. delivers.

As Shorty swings, he makes glancing contact. He hits a lazy pop-up to a slightly shifted Bucky in right center field for an easy out. Just as Bucky throws the can of corn in, one of the Trappers yells from their fragrant dugout that we have a real beaver playing right field. The Trapper is mocking Bucky's grill. Big Red snaps his eyes to the heckler and says, "That one is gonna cost you."

"How much?" a Trapper counterpart asks as the team laughs.

"All of you three dollar bills," says Red.

The umpire makes sure it doesn't go any further by forcing Pottsy to step up to the plate and continue the game. Red only makes fun of someone's features if they're surgical enhancements later in life done to draw more desirable attention, as with Mrs. Junker's clunkers. He may call you names that you bring on yourself, but it's never about something you inherited and can't control. Anyone who makes fun of someone else for something like that is likely to push his prime button by doing so.

With Pottsy now dug in, it smells like he must have sat directly on a spot of faux fox urine in the fox den dugout. I point to the middle of the field to alert our guys that Pottsy loves to go up the middle and try to decapitate his opponent. I call for another curve ball. J. J. sets, winds up, and delivers his second called ball. As I'm throwing the ball back, Pottsy says something about his fondness for fox urine.

"Don't know what you're talking about." I say as I squat down and call for another pitch.

"Sure you do." he says as he waits for the pitch.

"Strike one!" calls the ump.

Again, as I throw the ball back to J. J., Potts says, "Hey I know where I can get some black market fox pee if you're interested."

Thinking this is a hell of a conversation, I tell him, "Still don't know what you're talking about."

As he waits for his pitch, he says something about fox napping and selling bootleg fox pee. But the conversation is soon over. Pottsy makes contact on the next pitch. Jonas makes a diving stop up the middle and throws a laser over to first base for the third out, robbing Pottsy of a base hit.

I hear "All right, guys!" from the stands, along with a few whistles from the students sitting on top of their cars behind center field.

"Nice start out there," says Coach Gibbs's who is surprisingly congratulating every player coming off the field with a high five.

"Nice play, shortstop," says one of the scouts.

Going up to Jonas, I give a quick open palm to his rear hindquarter and say, "You can scratch the thought of anyone here talking about your shoes."

With a big grin he says, "Thanks, Fridge, and thanks for the advice on telling those head critics where to go."

"Always keep that ammo in your arsenal," I tell him.

Billy the batboy yells out the names of the first four hitters in order: "Motor, Junker, Mr. Ricky the Fridge Cooper, and McStein."

Another attribute that focused ball players possess is the ability to remember certain moments throughout the game that remind us of our importance. Hearing your name (in my case, my whole name, including title and nickname, thanks to Billy) read out loud when you come off the field is a great honor and reminds you of your responsibility and commitment to the team. Some teams forget to use this motivator and simply tape a lineup onto the inside of the dugout wall, which leaves room for laziness. Every door should be left open to keep the team's head in the game, which leaves much less room for error.

"Batter up!" yells the game caller.

"Motor," I say, as he's ready to leave the on deck circle.

"What's up, Fridge?" he asks.

"Don't overrun the bases," I warn him.

"No sweat, Fridge," he says with a slight chuckle, "I got this." He runs to the plate. While Motor's taking his stance, I hear the Trapper Skipper barking out orders from just outside the dugout. He's telling the corners to move up and guard against the bunt. Motor bats left handed but throws right handed. He made the switch over to the left side of the plate a few years back when he learned he could get a better jump from there and a better opportunity to round first for second. The majority of the time, he wants to lay a bunt down and have the infielders test his legs.

As he waits for the first pitch, I hurry out of my catcher gear to get a helmet on and to pick up the Hammer.

"Ball one!" I hear the umpire say.

"Hey, Fridge?" asks Red. "What was Potts jawing to you about out there?"

"Something about backdoor fox urine for sale," I say.

Gunner, standing just on the other side of me, speaks up. "Ya, my dad used to buy some of their underground piss by the gallon for a cheap price, but they were busted too many times for my dad's liking."

In the meantime, I hear a "Strike one!" call on Motor. As I step away from the ridiculous conversation to my batter's hole spot, I can still hear Red asking more about the black market operation. I refocus on Pottsy's arm instead of his illegal fox farm. I watch him deliver a decent changeup to a swinging and missing Motor. With the count one and two, I'm hoping Motor is sitting on a fast ball from Potts, who is already tipping his pitches.

As a batter, this is a crucial advantage to make an average hitter look like he knows what he's doing up there. If you're able to guess right on what type of pitch you're about to get, you should at least get a part of the bat on the ball. Great hitters who guess right should get the fat part of the bat on the ball. Exceptional hitters guess wrong and still find the sweet spot on both bat and ball.

Motor guesses right. He catches a piece of the outside fastball and bloops one over the third baseman's head. Rounding first, he would normally head for second, but Motor jams on the spike brakes and watches the baseball get picked up by the left fielder, who tosses it to second base for a lead-off single. For Motor to refrain from trying to turn the county leaguer into a close play at second base told all of us of his commitment to making a team effort.

With our lead-off man aboard, it was now J. J.'s turn at the plate. J. J. is a traditional righty. Everything he does is with his right hand. But J. J. has one thing that most of us righties could only dream of: a dominant left eye. He has led us in walks the past couple of seasons. He's a big reason I was able to post forty-four runs batted in last year, which in turn lead to higher scores and better opportunities for victory.

With J. J. now dug in, Pottsy wastes no time delivering four straight called balls for a free trip to first base for a select-eye hitter. Taking one last practice cut, I slam the top of the Hammer's handle on the ground to shake the weighted donut loose and take my walk up to the launching pad.

"Go get 'em," says Billy as he waddles back to the dugout with J. J.'s stick.

I acknowledge him with the wink of an eye.

Pottsy knows my history. I figure I won't see anything close to the strike zone. Except for a few echoes of encouragement, the closer I get to the box, the quieter the stands become.

As I reach the plate, I hold the Hammer in my left hand and my right fist in the air, asking for time to dig in. Permission from the umpire for extra time to settle in is not something you get unless you have earned it. As I dig my right foot in, I can hear the Trapper's manager barking orders for everyone to step back. I glance at the infield to see the third baseman damn near playing in the grass. This leaves the whole left side of the infield wide open for a bunt down the line.

More than anything, I would rather not do what I am about to do—but if I'm out here preaching about team commitment, I have to follow suit and lay down the advancement bunt. I'm now settled into my stance. The umpire motions to the pitcher to continue play.

Motor and J. J. take respectable leads, and I zero in on an inside fastball. As I wheel around to a bunt stance at the last second for contact, I hear some disappointment coming from the fans who are here to watch some long shots. Instead, I lay out a perfect bunt between the chalk and grass: a slow roller up the dirt.

Hustling down to first, I think about the conversation I had earlier with Miss Calculus and about how her grandfather gauged my speedometer. I envision him standing next to the bag with a stopwatch in hand timing my speed like a track coach next to the finish line. I see the first baseman stretching out from the bag. I know it is going to be a bang-bang play. But I have all pistons working and I accelerate through the bag before the ball reaches the southpaw's outstretched glove.

"Safe!" I hear the field ump yell, along with a chorus of cheers.

"Nice bunt, Fridge," Coach Jr. says as I walk back to the bag.

"Yeah, nice laser beam, Fridge," says the first baseman.

"Well, Captain Obvious…now, as you can see, we have a Beaver standing on every base, with zero outs and our cleanup man stepping up to the plate is hungry for some RBIs. This here in these parts is what we like to call baseball." Silence takes hold of his uneducated tongue.

Red makes his presence known, in particular to Miss Perfect, by looking like a lumberjack proud of his ax. He ambles to the box and steps in. Red's lumber seems small in his mammoth hands. Knowing Red, I can tell he is way too amped up to make a good decision. It doesn't take long for Pottsy to throw a curve ball past an over swinging leather splitter.

Coming back to first after my lead, I throw a spike in the dirt and shout out in frustration, "Come on, Red! Relax up there! You look like you're swinging on the runway over at the Crossroad County Airport!" Red's grimace cracks into a little smile.

Pottsy wastes no time toeing the rubber and delivering a pitch in the dirt, which Red lays off. "All right, Son, good eye up there," says Mr. McStein.

"Way to lay off," says Jonas, who is standing in the on-deck circle.

Pottsy then throws a hell of a changeup that could be called either way but is called outside for another ball.

"Get your pitch, Son," says the owner of the Irish Schnitzel.

"Rock and roll, Red!" shouted Mustang and his groupies occupying the center field fence.

Pottsy again delivers to a swinging Red, who just misses the high fastball. A good pitcher will follow up with the same pitch here, maybe even just a tad higher. For years, I've been telling Red this. I just hope he remembers.

As I take my lead again, Potts delivers the 2 and 2 count by throwing exactly what I thought past a patient Red. Now that Red has a full count and bases loaded, there is no room for a free base off Pottsy. The struggling pitcher catches the returning ball while simultaneously exhaling the word, "Shit."

This is the classic scene for the pitcher's best fastball, and a hitter knows what's coming. All of us base runners take our lead and wait for the verdict. No one speaks a word, but the air reeks of anticipation, along with the perspiration from the nearby dugout. Potts draws up enough nerve to rock into his motion and fire what everyone knows he is about to deliver.

Red shifts his two-hundred-and-fifty-pound frame forward and then back to his left side, loading up to unload. It reminds me of the Belgian pulling horse we worked with at Jonas's farm. When a pulling horse makes up his mind to pull, he leans all of his weight back toward what he's hooked to for a split second. When it leaps forward like a greyhound out of the gate, the push off the ground a Belgian will generate is something that you have to see to appreciate its willing heart.

Red unleashes his off-season full of hard work on the meaty fast-ball. He gives a grunt and then gives all of our Beaver faithfuls reason to believe in our community's quest to bring home the Tri-County trophy. The ball explodes off the barrel of the bat, and the players don't even bother moving from their spots. We all just watch it steadi-ly climb over our heads and continue to climb as it leaves the park.

Red's bomb ends with an explosion. His firework crashes through the back window of the Trapper's parked bus. Leave it to Red to pull something off like this. Most high school baseball players only dream of knocking a home run off the other school's bus, let alone sending one through the back window.

Running toward second, I look back at Red and shaking my head in disbelief. I damn near trip rounding the bag. As I pass the short-stop, I can see his eyes are still fixed on the wreckage.

"Ah, man," he says with a look of disbelief upon his face. Our center field party of student fans is now chanting, "Red! Red! Red!"

As I make the turn from third to home, Coach Gibbs is in the coaches' box trying to hide a grin. I glance at Pottsy before I set foot on home plate with the rest of the guys. He gives every indication that his next pitch is going to be a retaliating beanball. After touching the plate and scoring our third run, I high-five Motor and J. J. and turn around to see the reason for the pyrotechnic show we all just received.

"Is that better for ya, Fridge?" says Red as he is about to score.

"Yeah, Red," I say, "that's better."

As he crosses home plate, Red walks through a Beaver tunnel of super pumped players as though he just checked off another feat on his life accomplishment list. We are all reminded that it was Red who just pulled off another classic stunt and not some made-up action hero by the way he fumigates the tunnel of congratulators while say-ing, "Today's tray of beans packed a hell of lunch punch." The smell of Red's bean butt usually makes people take another route around the devastated area, but this time we are all bathing in our enjoyment of Big Red McStein.

"Jonas."

"Yes, Ricky?"

"The first pitch you see is going to be at your head, so bend at the knee and let it sail on over your helmeted head. After that, he should be willing to pitch to ya."

"Ok, Fridge," says Jonas while he pulls down on his helmet to make it a little more snug.

Walking back to the dugout with the crowd noise still up, I wink at Buzzy, who is just climbing into the on-deck circle, and say, "Here's your chance."

Setting up a bench clearing is the easiest and sometimes most necessary action to implement in baseball. In this case, all I have to do to is stoke the simmering fire in an already hotheaded Buzzy. For the most part, a tussle in the infield is just some pushing and pulling, along with a discussion of the attributes of the opposing players' mothers (poor J. J.) and maybe a sister or two. Only a couple of times over the years have I seen it lead to some swings and misses and some early showers, but nothing too serious.

"Hey guys, gather it in here," I say while standing in the middle of the dugout. I explain the situation we are about to be in and remind everyone to keep it as clean as possible. It's going to be a long season and we don't need any suspensions.

"Why now, Ricky?" asks Bucky.

"Because this will seal the deal on this crowd of ours coming back for more."

Coach Gibbs, already aware of what's coming, says while sitting at the end of the bench, "Absolutely no swinging of the fists out there. You hear me team?"

"Ya, Coach. What about swinging our ball bats at 'em?" Gunner says in a joking manner.

"Now damn it, Gunner, I'm serious here. We don't need any suspensions."

"Sure thing, Coach," replies a now straight-faced Gunner.

As the umpire gives the permission to play ball, the fans are still jacked about Red's bursting bomb and are now about to be sucked in with a finale. Just as I told Jonas, the pitcher sends the next ball on its way looking for Jonas's ear hole. Jonas does as he was told, and the ball goes over his head and slams into the backstop.

Buzzy is the first mad Beaver to cross the chalked line and go after the headhunter Trapper. The crowd goes silent as everyone stands, fear filling them with adrenaline. As a team, we all follow Buzzy's lead to the middle of the infield. On the way, I am doing my best to size up the situation. I guess I should have given this brawl a little more attention in the undercard. I can already see Buzzy balling up a fist in frustration as he squares off with Pottsy, who already has his glove off and is taking a bare-knuckle stance.

In any type of battle, once the enemy line is approached, a calm focused commander often must employ more than one maneuver in order to achieve victory while trying to defuse the situation. I'm throwing out orders to my men and focusing on blitzing Buzzy and the experienced Trapper. I know they'll be the most difficult to separate. I yell my hardest at Buzzy to pull back on the reins of his assault. My hardheaded comrade ignores my corner instructions and I see him try to unload a knockout punch to the chin of his opponent.

It's a good thing Buzzy's haymaker doesn't reach its final destination to the nerve just under Pottsy's chin. Instead, his right cross just barely grazes the bobbing and weaving Pottsy's cheek. There's a two-game suspension. Red and I are just about on them when I tell him, "Grab Buzzy, and I'll grab Pottsy."

As Pottsy returns fire, I am able to catch his elongated hook. I pull back on it and slide my hand up and around the back of the redneck while grabbing a handful of his belt. "Easy!" I shout, trying to get the two hotheads apart.

Red simply throws a bear hug around Buzzy's chest, thereby extinguishing the battle's main furnace before the opponents did some serious harm to one another. The rest of the squads were mostly playing "ring around the diamond" and throwing a few compliments to each other. Still trying to settle the pitcher down, I ask Pottsy if I could maybe get a gallon of his fox urine from his family's farm. Easing right up, he turns and says in a calm voice, "Sure thing, Fridge, and for you, I'll even throw in some spicy fox jerky."

Not really knowing how to respond to the order of urine I just made and the jerky I will get in the deal, I just nod my head and say, "Can't wait!"

Meanwhile, coaches and umpires are settling down the patty caking and the verbal abuse. The players remember the crowd is there to watch baseball, not a "beam a Beaver" game. The main umpire shouts, "Buzzy and Potts, you're both ejected from the game, and one more act of retaliation from either side will result in the game being called!"

"That could've been a lot worse," I think as I walk toward our dugout. It also educated me on the severity of calling for a bench-clearing crowd pleaser. Coach is about to lay into Buzzy for throwing a punch until I step in and take responsibility for my third baseman's actions. "Coach," I say as I throw my arm around my teammate, "Buzzy here didn't get the memo about not throwing any right crosses out there, because he wasn't in the dugout at the time you gave the order. He was warming up in the on-deck circle."

Still steaming, Coach throws two fingers out and says, "Two games, Buzzy. That move is going to cost you two games," and walks away.

"Thanks, Fridge, for handling Coach for me," says Buzzy.

"Thank you, Buzzy, for having the Amish kid's back out there. For now we'll just fill in Archie for ya at third, but I promise you that when your two-game suspension is over, you will have the third base bag back. In the meantime," I reach in my bat bag and pull out a thick book, "read this."

"What is it?" he asks.

"It's a book on anger management."

"What are you, Ricky Cooper, doing with a book like this?"

"Buzzy," I say, "you're not the only one with a temper."

By then, the student fans behind center are the only ones still chirping some smack talk, and we are almost ready to pick the game back up with Jonas at the plate with a 1 and 0 count. Since Potts got tossed, the new pitcher has to have a few warm up throws before the game can continue. I use this opportunity to make sure Jonas isn't rattled after being involved in his first bench clearing.

Walking halfway to the plate, I call his name, and he jogs over to me. As I see his face, I don't need to ask if he is good. The look he has tells me he is great. "Jonas, you're on your own up there against this guy," I say, pointing at the new pitcher, "I've never seen him pitch before."

"You know, Fridge, the way this guy's warming up reminds me of my dad's arm back at the farm."

"Right on," I say with a fist bump. "Continue to stand out, Jonas Kuber." I walk away.

In the distance, I can hear Daryl Drummer and his pep band warming up and trying to piece together some music. I can also hear laughter streaming from the children already playing their own game of mini Beaver ball behind the stands. Most parents already have a wide grin stenciled across their mugs. The concession stand soon wins the air quality battle against the fox by replacing the stench with the smell of buttered popcorn.

Every Beaver in the dugout has the same mission: to make this an undefeated season. The atmosphere reminds me of a Tri-County tournament game. Yet on paper, it's only a scrimmage.

The Stats

Jonas makes solid contact with the first pitch and ropes it over the third baseman's head and into the corner for his first double. That rest of the game, we never stop hitting. We yank most of the starters after the fourth inning, but not before we batted through the lineup three times.

J. J. pitches two shutout innings on one hit. His fastball never stops moving. If he's able to contain the pitch with his two off-speed pitches, batters beware of J. J. Junker. After we pull J. J., we stick Lefty in for a one base hit inning. He then hands the ball to his twin for an inning. Righty struggles with his command and walks the first two hitters he faces. But he and the backup catcher are able to find the umpire's strike zone and only surrender one run while leaving the bases full. Gunner rounds the game out for us by mowing down a rusty Trapper team.

I am proud of our defense. Our backup third baseman throws our only error of the game. Red would need a step ladder to catch the overthrow at first.

The defensive play of the game is in the first inning: Jonas's diving stop up the middle off Pottsy's hit. Jonas fine opening performance has the scouts asking, "Who the hell is this Velcro-shoe-wearing kid?" They are floored when they find out.

As for our team batting, I can't be any happier with the display we're putting on out there. Hits are contagious, and once you start putting a few together, no prescription from the opposition can counteract the confidence you carry with you to the plate. Motor holds true to his favorite saying, "I got this," by going 2 for 3, and two runs scored. J. J. accepts two walks and gives them an easily fielded ground out, finishing 0 for 1. Other than the base-hit bunt I put down in the first, the Hammer kisses a hanging curve ball, splitting center and right field for a standup double, scoring two. I finish 2 for 2 with a walk and two RBIs.

Big Red's second plate appearance results in a four-pitch strikeout. He is up there trying to knock off the man on the moon after his first performance. I have to remind him, "If you want to pretend you're swinging from an airport runway, land the plane. Don't take it up and away." His final at bat ends with a ricochet off the fence in left center, just missing another souvenir ball. Scoring me from second, he coasts into second for a two bagger. He finishes 2 for 3, driving in five.

Jonas again makes himself known by showcasing his natural ability to play the game. He is outstanding on both sides of the innings. For his offense, he has a double in the first, runs out a triple in his second at bat, and has a liner over the second baseman's head in his final plate appearance. I think about giving him the chance for the cycle with a fourth time up, but the season is long enough for plenty of opportunities for that milestone.

For the rest of the team, hits and RBIs are scattered, except for our DH'ing Herbie. The kid is showing a lot of poise and potential as a sophomore.

The umpires finally take the fox lickers off the grill by calling for the mercy rule after five innings. The score is Beavers 14, Trappers 1. Go Beavers!

7

"Nice job out there boys," says an old, deteriorating, sun-soaked farmer supporting a patched-up pair of coveralls while standing crooked against a straight fence.

"Thank you, sir," I reply with a tip of the cap.

As I walk out to slap the hand of the losers on the just-called game, I hear many of the fans showing their respect with congratulatory remarks and whistles of praise. It's always great to touch hands after a game as the winners, even if it's not for the record book. For the most part, the losing side walks with their heads down and with not a word to say. But when it's team rivals walking past each other in such close proximity, the comments exchanged make for great entertainment, at least if you're the team with the W.

This is where I shine. To be a winner, you have to seem borderline cocky to some people. However, sometimes it paints the wrong picture about a person's character, and others may think you're being an arrogant ass. I'm ok with a chippy kind of attitude. Like I said, some people need it to give you their utmost. On the other hand, when people outside your family talk about how well you play the game, there's no need to force the pride. When I'm shaking hands after a game, I believe both sides of the line should show respect. If they don't, I make sure they don't forget by handing out a few truth-ful remarks that may hit some folks in their blind spots.

"See you guys in Fox Lake," says the first Trapper coming through the loser line.

"Twelve days, twenty-one hours, and counting down till you get to touch Beaver Ball winners' hands again, so cheer up," I say.

The next Trapper to slap hands is Shorty Glover, who doesn't ut-ter a sound. You have to respect a quiet loser—his brain controls his tongue. The next in line is one of their battered pitchers. The silence is soon broken by the Trappers' first baseman, whose comment earns him the obvious idiot award. I actually stop and ask him if he could repeat what he just stuttered. Sure enough, he is able to sound out every muttered word just as if it had been recorded:

"N-n-next time we're gonna give you B-b-beavers a good l-l-licking."

Feeling a tad bad for the impaired comment I say, "You know, one bag, Beaver Falls High offers some great tutors." He stands dumbfounded. I give him the benefit of the doubt and simply ask him, "Have you ever licked a beaver?"

Some of our guys and a couple of theirs overhear the conversa-tion, making for good humor down the line until I reach Pottsy. He serves up the top-shelf shot of the day by claiming, "I've licked a beaver or two."

After the entertaining mandatory slaps of thanks for showing up are over, I spot my dad talking to Mrs. Perfect's male companion. It doesn't take long for Red to notice the beauty standing behind the two. He slaps me on the elbow and asks, "You know anything I don't?"

"No," I say, "but I'm about to find out."

"What do you think she'll say?" he asks.

"For your diploma," I reply.

"Hey, Dad," I say as I approach him and the medium-sized guy.

Dad says to Red and me, "Hey guys, nice game today. The team looks solid out there. It was great to see everyone contributing. Red, way to park it in the first." Dad can tell I want to be introduced to the middle-aged guy standing next to him, so he formally introduces Red and me to "Mr. Joe Average."

Recognizing the name of another retired major league player, I waste no time extending my paw for a firm shake from the average Joe. "Thanks for showing up today, sir," I say while still shaking his medium-sized hand.

"It's been my pleasure seeing you play the game of baseball the way it's meant to be played, Ricky Cooper." Letting go, he turns to his left and says, "This here is my lovely wife, Mrs. Average."

Red about chokes on his own saliva at the introduction. Not because she is married, but rather the fact that someone so perfect could have such an average name.

"Please, call me Jane," she says as she steps closer with her hand extended just the way princesses do. Feeling Red's emotions take control of him, I take the time to gently caress her soft hand before he could smear a pair of salted lips and possibly a slip of the tongue upon it.

"Ma'am," I say with a nod of my head the way gentlemen do. Then, after a brief moment, I let go of her no-need-for-lotion hand and turn to Mr. Average, waiting for him to continue.

"Ricky, I'm here today representing the Royal Crowners out of Shottsville. We would like, one of these near evenings, to sit down with you and your family over dinner and talk about the possibility of joining one of the most winning organizations in the history of game. Your dad here tells me you haven't committed yet to any of the wheelbarrow load of offers that's been dumped on your doorstep."

"Thanks for the recognition sir, but the wheelbarrow has only dumped next level offers," I say.

"Well, Ricky, that's all about to change for you, now that you're a senior. I just want the first crack at landing you in a Royal Crowners' jersey."

I'm astonished. I can only say, "That's been part of my dream, to make it to the highest level of baseball. Thank you, Mr. Average... and Jane," acknowledging the perfect half of the Averages.

"You're quite welcome," the beauty responds. "I'll see you back at the car," she tells her husband, turns, and walks away, leaving Red with a drooling chin.

"So, Mr. Cooper, why don't you and I talk here and let these boys get back with the team?" says Mr. Average.

"Yeah, sure thing," says Dad. "Son?"

"Ya, Dad?"

"Congratulations on the first victory of the young season," and with a father-son fist bump of trust, he adds, "Your mother and I will see you later at the Irish Schnitzel."

"Later, Mr. Cooper."

" Later, Red."

Just as we turn our backs and walk off, we hear, "Hey, meat eater." We turn to look back at all five feet and eight inches of Mr. Joe Average. "You keep eating those baseballs up there at the plate. In the future, you'll also be able to afford the nicest cuts of meat."

"Oh, hell yeah!" says Red.

"Classic," I hear my dad say.

As we make our way back to the rest of the team, Red says, "It's a good thing, Fridge, you snapped up Mrs. Perfect's precious hand before I could get my lion paw on that rare fillet."

"My pleasure, Red. Besides, your eyes damn near burned a hole through her."

"Yes, Fridge, you're right. But remember: I'm not only a talent judge for showroom models but also the leader of the team in home runs this year."

"You just keep doing what you're doing and I'll embrace the hand of your judged models," I replied back.

"Hey, Cooper," I hear from the opposite side of the field.

There, standing just outside the visitors' dugout is Pottsy. He's waving me over and saying, "Come here."

"Shit, I was hoping he forgot about that," I say.

"What the hell does he want?" asks Red.

"While I was breaking up him and Buzzy, I kinda ordered a gallon of fox urine."

"Why in Trapper's hell did you order a gallon of the stuff when a few drops does the trick?"

"Maybe I want to take up fox trapping," I say with a smirk. "Now come on. You're going with me." We change our route.

As we take the long way to get to where Pottsy is standing, I am trying to think quickly how I can cancel my order, but too soon Red and I are standing across from the criminal.

"Hey, Cooper. Is the big guy cool?" he asks, pointing and referring to Red.

"Hell yeah, I'm cool, you bootlegging piss farmer," says Red.

"With that kind of attitude, I assume you've bought illegally before," says Pottsy.

I take control of the matter and answer before Red can. "Say, Pottsy," I begin, "about the conversation we had out there during the bench clearing—"

Before I can finish, Pottsy interrupts. "My pa has a couple extra gallons in the back of the station wagon and is ready to make the transfer."

"Transfer?" I ask.

"Yeah, Cooper, the sale of illegal urine for green paperbacks," says Red while slapping me on the back.

"Actually, guys," says Pottsy, "ever since my grandpappy started the piss-farming business, the first gallon is on the farm, so there's no money needed today: I just need to know where you want it stashed."

Red dives back in and says, "Tell your kin to set it under the tall oak tree among the pines on the way out of the parking lot."

"Ok," says Pottsy. "Tall oak tree. Got it."

"By the way, Pottsy," I say, "What's the best use for the stank stuff?"

"You mean other than dumping some in the visitors' dugout?" he asks.

"Still don't know what you're talking about," I say.

"Yes you do, Cooper, but I think by now you understand my liking for the scent, so thanks for the welcome dousing in there," he says, pointing to the visitors' dugout. "Anyways, the best use is to put it around a trap. It helps coax in the sly fox by making him relax before he finds himself caught in a snare."

"Ha! Surprised you didn't know that, Fridge," says Red.

"I'm not surprised you did, Red," I reply.

"All right, guys, I gotta go. That's the old man's wagon horn a-blowing. Enjoy the pee." And off walks the rightful heir to the only known underground family fox urine farm bootlegging salesman.

"I feel like a criminal," I say to Red as we walk back to our own dugout.

"Don't sweat it, Fridge. It's just a gallon of liquid. Besides, it's not like you exchanged anything for it."

"Maybe a bit of pride," I say.

Jonas is the first one to greet us as Red and I approach the dugout. Jonas is grinning ear to ear, with his hand held high for a five-finger slap from his teammates.

"Greatest day of my life," he says while letting out the emotions that have been building up.

"You've only just begun, my friend," I tell him.

Grinning even wider, he says something in German that I assume means how excited he is.

The next duty of a team captain is to keep building confidence in your guys. A simple "Nice snag!" or "Nice toss!" or "Good wood out there today!" is all that's needed in most cases. Some minds need a bit more attention, while with a select few, you need not say anything. The best way to fill up someone's self-esteem and praise tank is to do it individually.

First up is Junker, who is loading up his bat bag. "Nice all-around performance, J. J.," I say.

Looking up he says, "Thanks, Fridge," and goes right back to the task at hand.

Next up is Righty, who's sitting down and changing out of his spikes. "Hey, Righty," I say, "Nice job regaining your command there in the fourth inning."

"Yeah, I was about to give up on trying to locate the fastball until I remembered I had a touch of udder balm under the tip of my cap."

"Whatever it takes," I say. I get a quick fist bump and move on.

Motor is standing next to the water cooler. "Say, Legs."

"What's up, Fridge?"

"Watching you run out there never gets old. Humans have played the game of ol' stick and ball for a long time. Not many have had the extra gear you have under the hood. Keep up the good work at the plate and you'll continue to have the opportunity to showcase your rare gift." A slight grin and a laugh are all I need to know that Motor has this.

"Archie."

"Hey, Fridge."

"Nice job filling in for Buzzy on the corner and nice patience with the bat."

"Thanks, Fridge."

Billy, our bat boy, was waiting patiently until I was done congratulating Archie's performance. "Um, Fridge?" he says

"Attaboy, Billy." I high-five the little chub for calling me Fridge. "Whatcha need?" I ask.

"There are some scouts on the fence just outside the dugout asking to see you and Lefty."

"How many?" I ask.

"I counted seven guys total," he says while holding seven fingers.

I smile and say, "Thanks for your help today, Billy." I reach into my back pocket, pull out an open bag of sunflower seeds, and toss it underhand to him. "Billy, there's one more thing." I send him on a mission and move to encourage the next player. A simple fist bump is all Herbie, our promising sophomore, needs as I walk by.

Gunner is next in line. As I get to him he's putting some kind of powder on his right elbow. "Gunner," I say, "I've got a favor to ask you."

"Anything, Fridge."

"You know how Pottsy's family business of delivering goods works, right?"

"Yeah, I was a part of the pickups in my early learning days in the backseat of a four-wheel drive."

"All right," I say "you've got another pickup to make."

After a short explanation, I continue down the line, right past Bucky. Sometimes it's interesting talking to the future chemist, but not about baseball. He applies science into everything, including how to play ball.

"Hey, Fin," I say, "You see Buzzy?"

"He's already hit the shower."

"Coach know?" I ask.

"Yeah, he's the one who sent him there."

"Good move," I say. "The quicker Buzzy cools off in a cold shower, the better."

Lefty is sitting next to my bat bag. He's changing into his low-cut, leather barn boots while still sporting a baseball uniform. I pop a squat next to him on the pine. It doesn't take long for us to start talking about the scouts standing outside our dugout.

Lefty asks, "What's the possibility of an Elite-level scout being out there?"

I'm not sure if Mr. Joe Average was sent here by the brass to show interest in just me or in Lefty as well, so I dodge the question by offering him one of the two half-melted chocolate bars from inside my bat bag. Chocolate has a way of helping out in many different circumstances, and it gave me enough time to say "Billy said there are seven guys standing out there waiting on us."

As we each take a huge bite of the milk chocolate, our senses shift to simple enjoyment. We both recline back against the bench. "You've gotta love it," says Lefty.

"Yes, you do," I say with a mouthful of sweetness. "You can almost taste a hint of salt," I add.

"Actually, Fridge, I was referring to the seven scouts," he says.

"Yes," I reply "how sweet it is." We sit there for a moment not saying a word. Both of us are just running through all the possibilities.

"Lefty," I say, breaking the silence, "no matter where our careers lead us, let's never forget this moment of innocence."

"What do mean, Fridge?" he asks.

"Careers lead even the smallest of homegrown, small-town graduates into ways of life away from their roots. I pause to take another bite while studying the field in front of us. "They say it's easy to become mesmerized by the bright neon lights pointing you there and telling you, 'Come in here.' In Crossroad County, we still use simple signs hung from the inside of a window or doors letting outsiders know the hours of business or simply when we're around. Our streets aren't lined with maximum-wattage lamp posts that make even the darkest night bright. You can easily lose sight of the simple things in life when shiny new things are placed in front of you. So whether it would be—"

"Fridge, I don't mean to interrupt you, but it sounds like you're writing a book of analogies," says Lefty.

Smirking, I say, "Just maybe." After another minute of silence, I backhand his kneecap with my knuckles while getting up and saying, "It's going to be a great season."

Coach is just shoring up the final stats with Coach Jr. when I approach the two. "Coach," I say, "you gotta minute?" He never really likes to say much after a game while still at the field. His postgame rant, if he has one, is always reserved for the locker room.

"Yes, Ricky, I do." He gets up and walks to the opposite side of the dugout. I follow him past where the recruitment hunters are standing as they wait for their shot at bagging a trophy. "You and the men played a nice game today," he says as we stop just outside the corner of the hut.

"Yes sir, we did," I say. "The overall character of the bunch is high on winner's commitment."

Grinning, he says, "Ricky Cooper, you would make a fine general."

"I love to lead, Coach," I respond.

He gives another slight grin as he asks, "So, what's this conference for?"

"Coach, did you know about the major league scout who was here for the game?"

"No, Ricky, I didn't. Who is he representing?"

"The Royal Crowners of Shottsville," I answer.

A brief pause from Coach indicates he is proud of that fact.

"Joe Average is the gentlemen's name," I add.

"Ricky, I knew the day would arrive when you were going to have to make a decision about what level of baseball you wanted to continue playing. You have everything necessary to make the correct call. Life's obstacles occur on and off the field. You will need to choose what to do. Most young men who have a third of your opportunities make decisions based on themselves at the time and forget to look beyond the moment. There's not a doubt in my mind, Ricky, that whatever decision you make, it'll be what's best for you and those around you."

Hearing these words of praise coming from a man of few words is more inspiring than he may realize. Eye to eye, player to coach, I say "Thank you." He turns to walk away. "Coach, there's one more thing that I'd like you to explain."

"Yes?" he says.

"Ever since I was a freshman, you would preach to the team—especially the older ones—about never having a girlfriend during baseball season."

"Yes."

"Why?"

"Ricky, Walter Rawlings's granddaughter would make a fine girlfriend for you." My look of surprise makes Coach answer the question I hadn't asked: how did he know?

He says, "By maintaining focus on my surroundings."

As he walks away, I stand there thinking, "Here I am, still in uniform, in my favorite environment, just after a win, and I'm focusing on Miss Calculus."

I'm soon pulled back into a baseball frame of mind by the hooting, hollering, and good-bye waves coming from our center field gallery of student fans. They're wishing the Trappers of Loss Lake a safe trip home on a bus full of broken glass. I can hear the players, all of them, sitting toward the front of the wreckage, yelling something about fresher air quality, a thousand-acre lake they have, and to enjoy our dammed up river full of beavers. They don't seem to be buying the fans' wishes for their safe trip home.

"What a great way to start the season," says Red as he approaches me from behind. We both stand there looking out at the ship leaving port for a moment, only to laugh at the banana skin someone on the bus tosses out and the slew of middle fingers waving side to side. "A little childish," I say.

"Would you expect anything less?" says Red.

"Not a bit."

"Look at Billy Belly waddling this way," is the next comment from Red.

Looking over, I see Billy walking down left field with one arm full of hot dogs and another full of cola cans. "What's he doing?" asks Red.

"He's doing what I asked of him," I say with a smile.

"Fridge, you keep storing food like you do, you're gonna need a helping hand out of that catchers squat of yours."

Adjusting my jock, I tell him, "Don't worry, I'll save room for the Schnitzel's special later."

Billy reaches us in a moment. He managed to carry three dogs and three colas down from the center field tailgaters who were packing leftovers away and giving some out. "Good job, Billy," I tell him.

"You're welcome, Mr. Cooper. As soon as I told them it was for you, they loaded me up with this," he says as he shows us.

"Perfect," I say. "Two dogs and two colas for me and one of each for you, Billy."

"Thanks, Mr. Fridge," says the tubby boy as he walks away with a hot dog and bun in his mouth.

Red only holds out for a moment. "Damn it, Fridge, give me one of those imitation links."

I hand him both a dog and cola and say, "You're right, it's no Schnitzelwurst, but we are at a ballpark celebrating a win," as I "cheers" my hot dog with his.

"Red," I say between bites, "on paper, Easton Prep is slated for another trophy, especially with the addition of Bo." I pause for another bite "But we have the team to win it all. Shit, even Buzzy's on board." Throwing down the last bite of mystery meat and a quick rinse of sugary soda, I say, "Everyone but Lefty."

"What do mean?" asks Red.

"His sights are already beyond high school ball."

"What makes you think that?" he asks around a mouthful.

"It turns out my friend, that you and ol' Buzzy were right. Lefty and his brother should have dragged Jonas with them for his knowledge of utters to any live teet auction, if that's where they were really going."

"I'm not sure I follow ya, Fridge."

"Let me explain what gave it away. First, we know the Oliver's place is close to the Kuber farm. It has never been an issue to pick up and drop off Jonas the times I've done it. Today felt no different, because the Olivers supposedly had auction duty for the family yanking business. Even when Jonas and I pulled into the student parking lot this morning and you and he exchanged pleasantries.

But then, during lunchtime, Buzzy made the same comment that the Olivers should have taken Jonas with them and was surprised they didn't. Buzzy's attitude is piss poor right now, but I do need to do a better job of understanding the issues he faces. Nothing sank in until Lefty walked into the locker room wearing his usual cowboy get up and a fancy pair of metal-tipped boots."

"He wears those boots a lot," says Red.

"Yes, but never around a bunch of other farmers in a sale barn."

"You've got a point there," says Red. "Maybe he changed into his fancy-dancy leathers after they left the auction."

"Yes, but when he walked in, he was also empty handed. His bat bag was still hanging in the locker from the day before. The proof of his guilt was unveiled when, after the game, he pulled his well-worn barn boots out of his bat bag and slipped 'em on."

"Guilty of what?" asks Red.

"Guilty of making up an excuse and covering up the real reason for him not being where he said he was."

"You're basing this on the man's boots?"

"Shoes, my friend, are a great indicator of what a man does and where he's been."

After sucking down the rest of his cola, Red asks, "Where do you think he was then?"

"Don't know. But wherever it was, he doesn't want his teammates to know."

"What the..." says Red. I look where he's looking. I'm little stunned, too, but I'm also excited.

My half-ton pickup never looked so good. Sitting there on the tailgate, with her dangling legs swinging back and forth, is a picture pasted forever in my mind.

"Is that who I think it is?" asks Red.

"Sure is," I say, with my eyes still glued on the prize.

"What, are you getting tutoring later?"

Grinning, I say "Maybe. Red, I'll see you up at the locker room."

"Why?" he asks.

"Because I'm about to get a date for the senior prom."

"By all means, *Romeo*. Have at it, but just remember there's gonna be some wet Beavers crying over Ricky Cooper's pick of the litter for prom."

"Exactly why I'm not wasting another moment to ask my first choice."

"Don't you think you might want to get a shower first?"

"No, I'm good, Red. Besides, this catch has a fondness for a gritty baseball player. See you up there, Red," I say as I point to the school's locker room and grab a fist bump.

"Good luck, Juliet," he replies, walking on.

With most of the guys, including Red, already heading up to the boy's shower to erase the dirt from their skin, I finish up packing my gear into my bat bag. Leaving the dugout, I walk toward my half-ton pickup sitting about seventy-five yards away in the student parking lot. My feet never felt so light; maybe it is my heart feeling lighter because I am about to open it up and share it.

I've had a few acquaintances in the past. Mostly tagalong cheerleaders set up by Big Red and his significant other to round out a double date. Nothing against the other girls, but this moment feels true to the organ beating in my chest.

I know exactly—word for word—what I'm going to say. It's as if I am about to recite a poem being released by each beat under my left pectoral. The closer I get, the slower she swings those slightly tanned legs and the more I forget the poem I was set to deliver.

I approach her. She's smiling the whole time, showing those pearly whites. I say nothing about the rehearsal. I just extend a fist for a bump back and say, "Nice performance, Grace."

"Ricky Cooper," she says, "I wasn't sure if you knew my real name or not."

She was right. Not that I didn't know her true name, but I never spoke it aloud. I might have thought it silently in my mind but never let it roll off the tip of my tongue and into the open air. "I'm sorry, Grace, for never calling you by the name your parents gave you," I say to her. "I've learned a lot about you today, and now my focus is set on learning more…I mean, if you'll let me."

As the tears well in her eyes, so do the emotions in my heart. She slides off the tailgate and quickly wraps her long arms around me. "You had a nice performance, too."

I realize that I'm standing there with my bat bag in hand. I fix that problem right away by dropping it and gently but firmly wrapping my arms and hands around her waist. Ok, maybe just a little lower.

It feels like I am making up for lost time on a long-overdue caress and hug. Within a few seconds of being lost in the moment, I soon discover the discomfort of being aroused while housed in a supported shell protector. I call "timeout," readjust, and then dive back into those arms as Grace giggles.

Love has a funny way of revealing itself at the opportune time. Here's a girl I've known since kindergarten, through the years of elementary, middle school, and then high school. Except for our tutoring sessions, I've barely ever spoken to her outside the classroom until now. And here she is wrapped up in my arms, breathing against my neck. Backing off a little but still holding on, I say, "Miss Cal—" and then stop myself. "Grace, I assume you don't have a date to prom yet, right?"

"Actually, I do," she says. "His name is Ricky Cooper."

What a preseason!

11 - 11 - 16

ABOUT THE AUTHOR

Erich Johann Haas is a barber by trade. Between haircuts, he exercises his thoughts with a stroke of the pencil as he writes the second book in this series of three. Outside the shop, he enjoys a round of golf and being in the presence of his family, who live comfortably in Carroll County, Ohio.

Made in the USA
Middletown, DE
28 March 2016